THE BRINK

OF

CHAOS

By

Eric Richardson

To Grandma and Grandad,

Eric ☺

British Library Cataloguing In Publication Data
A Record of this Publication is available
from the British Library

ISBN 1846853974
978-1-84685-397-5

First Published 2006 by

Exposure Publishing, an imprint of Diggory Press,
Three Rivers, Minions, Liskeard, Cornwall, PL14 5LE, UK
WWW.DIGGORYPRESS.COM

For my brother, Sean, who provided so much inspiration for this book.

. Chapter One .

A HERO FALLS

UNQUIN was surrounded by a crazed inferno. He plunged his axe into yet another of his enemy. As the mighty weapon made impact, Unquin glimpsed his friend Zuboko torching a foul orc that was brandishing a large rusted sword; the orc was sent fleeing from the besieged village, squealing in pain and agony.

Meanwhile Aerlyn, in the thick of the battle, released two scorching arrows which found their mark in the chests of two unsuspecting gnolls. Both dropped their weapons and crashed to the ground.

Harthor's mighty long sword sliced through a warty goblin's neck making a sickening crunch as it separated head from body. As the head rolled down the muddy embankment Harthor brought down the blood stained sword on the next goblin who fancied his chances against the mighty cleric. Bewilderment gazed up from the goblin's eyes as he was skewered. Green ooze spewed from his toothless mouth and he dropped to his knees.

Human screams rang out from the village huts as a marauding ogre scorched the thatched roofs and waited to impale the victims as they fled from the scorching heat and the belching, poisonous smoke. He stabbed a crying child and a fleeing mother.

"Amundin!" cried Zuboko, enraged, as a blinding light from the mighty staff of the half orc shamen pierced the eyes of the demented ogre. The ogre continued to thrash blindly, but he was vulnerable now. With a resounding thud the ogre fell to the ground, sprawling onto the burning embers, two sacred arrows quivered in his back. Aerlyn had made her mark again.

Unquin hacked his dwarven axe into a leather clad orc, immediately disembowelling him. The orc stood, amazed, watching his insides falling to the ground; moments later he too fell to the ground amongst his innards.

Unquin never heard the lumbering bulk crashing down towards him. Hard in battle he never felt the ground shake as it charged. It was a humongous, hideous troll; thick moss like growths covered his muscular back, muscles rippled beneath his leathery skin. Its arm was raised, poised for attack.

"Unquin!" screamed Harthor, watching in apparent slow motion, unable to defend Unquin, his fellow hero. The arm slammed into the unsuspecting Unquin. The pure strength of it lifted him high in the air smashing bones on impact. It was a mortal blow.

If Unquin had lived, he would have witnessed Harthor charge the repulsive troll. Revenge for the death of his gnomish friend ravaged Harthor's eyes and gave him the strength of ten brutish men. The troll, unsteadied by the charge teetered backwards, stumbling over a blood stained corpse. The troll's arms flailed in a vain attempt to keep standing. With a thundering crash he hit the ground. Harthor, at full speed, sailed through the air and landed full force on the troll's broad chest. Two hands clasped tight to his mighty sword and Harthor plunged it hard into the chest of the hideous troll.

Harthor thought he had finished the troll as he was not aware of the strange healing ability that all trolls possessed. No sooner had Harthor removed his bloody sword than the gaping wound he had made started to heal itself. The troll, fully healed, opened its three bloodshot eyes and struggled to its feet. Luckily for Harthor, Zuboko had encountered these mighty beasts before and was prepared for its self healing. Already a swirling cloud storm was surrounding Zuboko as he conjured up a fire spell and unleashed it at the troll. It hit the troll square in the chest and consumed him with a flaming fireball. The troll roared and turned to ash.

As the pieces floated to the ground the battling orcs, goblins, ogres and gnolls realised that their mighty ally had fallen. Panic spread through their ranks and then fear. Ear piercing screeches rang through the evening air as each dark warrior fled to the safety of the mighty oaks.

The heroes seized their chance to make a massive impact on the marauders. Zuboko raised his arms. Jewelled fingers spread towards the fleeing crowds. A sea blue beam of lightning erupted from each gnarled nail. The beams flashed across the battlefield each finding a victim. As each beam made its deadly contact the unsuspecting beasts dropped to the earth, eyes wide open. No wounds. No blood, but all the life force sucked away.

At the same time Harthor unlatched his holy crossbow from his back. He recited a prayer and fired a wooden stake at an unfortunate goblin who had almost reached the safety of the oaks. The shot was precise and fatal, impacting the gap between its crude and gnarled armour and its protectively spiked helmet. The dark creature gargled and slumped to its knees.

The path to the forest was now littered with bodies. Aerlyn let loose twenty arrows upon the left flank of troops, felling trolls and goblins. None missed. The heroes had defeated vast numbers of the dark warriors but it was too late to destroy them all. The survivors were already scrambling into the dense undergrowth where they would be protected by the defences of the impassable forest.

Aerlyn and Harthor dropped their weapons and whirled round to see their noble friend, Unquin, lying on the cold brick doorstep of a desolate house. He was ashen. Around him lay the bodies of his enemies, all with axe shaped wounds. He had fought a brave battle to the last. His last breath had been witnessed by no-one, he had died alone.

Villagers frantically tried to extinguish the blazing fires, tend the wounded, locate their loved ones and salvage their belongings. The village was devastated. A village medic came scurrying over in response to Aerlyn's anxious cries. His dark cloak smeared with the blood of those he had already tended. A large crucifix hung around his neck. The tiny man examined Unquin's lifeless body and shook his head, confirming to the heroes that their companion was no more. Aerlyn was blinded by tears; Harthor made a cross sign to his chest and bowed his head. Zuboko, overwhelmed with loss, fainted.

Aerlyn and Harthor struggled through the debris, helping Zuboko towards the makeshift hospital. They had all been injured. Zuboko's thigh was bleeding heavily following a massive onslaught by a gnoll veteran with a large scythe. Aerlyn had suffered a deep slash on her chest when she had lost her balance jumping from a burning cottage. Harthor's armour had protected him from most damage but his forearm bore a small injury where he had taken on a goblin spearman.

None of the companions had emerged unscathed from the fierce encounter.

. Chapter Two .

THE COMING OF CHAOS

IT WAS the morning after the devastating battle. Harthor was still dressed in full battle body armour, smeared with mud and the blood of both foe and friend. The smell of death was all around. Frantically doctors and nurses tried to save their patients although resources were low and many suffered.

"How is she?" Zuboko asked Harthor when they were at the medics. "She hasn't spoken all day," replied Harthor.

Zuboko laid a heavy hand on his fellow hero, Harthor, and made his way out, wearily, to sit with Aerlyn.

Zuboko, a half orc druid from the barren mountainous area of Hoggrack, had been outcast from the village as a child and had made himself a solitary life high in the mountains. The villagers had been fearful of his appearance. A genetic throwback had resulted in his having the physical appearance of an orc; dark brown, leather like skin with the magical markings of the chaos god Ladracksin. His face was distorted by fibrous growths, one of which had partially blinded his right eye and further disfigured his already ugly face. Zuboko's magical ability had been with him since birth and each day his powers grew ever stronger. At all times he carried with him his sacred staff, crudely made and decorated with the skull of his first kill, a bugbear. Many feared him on sight, but he was a loyal comrade to those few who knew him well.

As he strode over to where Aerlyn sat, his mind was racing. "Hey Aerlyn," Zuboko murmured.

He'd finally found Aerlyn at the burial site where now at least twenty women and children sat crying and wailing over the graves of their loved ones, struck down in battle the previous night. A thick cloud of grey smoke smothered the sky like rust on an old shield. Aerlyn was crouched by a tall statue; a statue of Unquin, bearing the terrible axe of dwarves. Her eyes were swollen and bloodshot; tears flowing freely down her pale cheeks.

Aerlyn was of royal blood; she had been born a wood elf and therefore possessed grace and agility but was also endowed with the ability to perform enchantments with the use of her staff, an ancient artefact passed down through many generations from the very first wood elves. She was six thousand and thirty one years old, was well practised in the arts of archery and was a valuable member of the group. Aerlyn also worshipped the god of grace – Nemea - and had dedicated her life to hunting and destroying the chaos god – Ladracsin - and his servants, in an effort to maintain peace and tranquillity.

As Zuboko approached closer he recognised the elven display of grief as blue lightning sparks cascaded from Aerlyn onto the last remaining symbol of the great hero, Unquin, his statue.

"Leave me alone," grumbled Aerlyn in a hushed tone.

"But I just wanted to . . ." Zuboko started, wanting to support his companion as she had supported him so many times before. Zuboko would never forget Aerlyn's loyalty to him and the trust she placed in him. Aerlyn had stayed by Zuboko's side even when he had been accused of being the twenty first counsellor of chaos and in the service of Ladracsin.

"Leave me ALONE!" Aerlyn yelled menacingly. As she glared up at Zuboko her eyes changed a hue of colours and the red symbols of chaos flashed on her elegant palms.

Zuboko was familiar with the elven chaotic state and as requested stayed back. The balance between good and evil had been upset causing minor chaotic incidents; it was a fact of magic. They only happened for a few seconds during extremes of emotion and Aerlyn was soon apologising to her friend.

"I'm sorry," pleaded Aerlyn to Zuboko when she had passed the chaotic moment.

Together they made their way back to the hut where they had stored their weapons. Harthor had gone out to search for any clues from the attack. The night had quickly drawn in and the fire glowed and crackled.

"Aerlyn, the chaotic episode . . . why?" asked Zuboko. "The balance is upset?"

"Yes, it can only be one thing, Ladracsin!" Aerlyn whispered; they both looked at each other in anguish.

Ladracksin was the arch enemy of Nemea. He was pure evil.

Many years ago Ladracsin had been banished by Nemea to the nether realms of fire and darkness. Once he tried to break free from his shadowy tomb, forming armies of orcs and trying to destroy all that was elvish. The elves had emerged victorious but in trapping Ladracsin, Nemea had been wounded. She suffered a severe laceration to the forearm which, although successfully healed, had nonetheless left all elves with a permanent legacy of Ladracsin's evil; this meant that at times of extreme anger or sadness, elves were no longer able to control their chaotic side and were liable to attacks of uncontrolled rage and fury.

Zuboko hastily strapped his woolly, tattered sack to his belt and snatched his staff from under the ragged mattress while Aerlyn rushed out of the dilapidated hut, bow in hand.

"We must find Harthor!" Aerlyn yelled desperately.

In the distance, an almighty sound of clashing steel could be heard. A sudden roar scattered startled birds into flight.

A figure, dressed in black, dashed out of an alley brandishing a large broad sword. Zuboko, without hesitation punched the man to the ground. Surely this dark man had something to do with the whereabouts and disappearance of Harthor. The man lay on the ground, nose bloody and dazed by the sudden attack. Zuboko poised ready to strike again, faltered at the howl from the wounded man.

"Hey, steady big guy!" he stuttered. "I'm no threat to you. I'm a farmer. Didn't you hear that wolf howl? I have to protect my animals or the wretched beast will steal them all!"

"Sorry," mumbled the apologetic wizard, holding out a gnarled hand to help the farmer back to his feet.

The farmer clutching his nose stumbled to his feet. "I must protect my animals." He grabbed his sword, turned and ran into the darkness. Zuboko and Aerlyn looked at each other and sprinted into the darkness after the farmer.

As they ran they heard a sinister whistling, whizzing sound. Silver stakes soared through the air, followed by splattering sounds. In front of them came another sinister sound. Something ominous trundled menacingly through the starlit village. The sound was getting closer; sickening thuds and the crunch of smashing bones. The instant blood splattered on Zuboko's legs he realised what was the cause of the disturbance.

"Bugbear!" yelled Zuboko.

There was a terrible roar as the creature came into view. "No enter!" the bugbear bellowed from the pit of its enormous chest.

Warty lumps of pustulous pimples and wild fur smothered the beast's brutish muscles. A large spiked mace, smeared with blood, was gripped menacingly in a clawed fist. Lodged dramatically in the creature's shoulder was a sword of some description, so deeply embedded it was undistinguishable.

With the utmost speed Aerlyn had harnessed her bow and released a glistening arrow that trailed a sparkling, silver glow, straight at the beast's black, terrible heart. It seemed to do very little other than bounce off the beast's remarkably tough hide.

"So be it," the bugbear said grinning a vile grin. A fang stuck from its upper lip. The fell beast thundered down the cobbled road and crashed its deadly weapon at Zuboko. With surprising agility, Zuboko pulled a knife from his belt, dodged to the left and at the same time jumping. Zuboko then plunged the blade into the bugbear's pulsating jugular. The stunned beast stopped in its tracks and dropped to its knees as blood spurted from its neck with every beat of its evil heart. Zuboko landed cat like, pulled the sword from the bugbear's shoulder and masterfully thrust the metal into the beast's gut. Aerlyn unlatched another arrow, blue fire sparked the tip and it sailed towards the now blood smothered organs of the bugbear. With no further sounds the obnoxious creature slammed forwards into a blood bath, dead.

Catching his breath, Zuboko released the sword admiringly from the beast's gut, "I think I'll have this."

"I think I've found the farmer," Aerlyn said in dismay. The farmer's mangled body was strewn across a stone wall. Barely recognisable, the almighty thrash of the bugbears' mace had ended his life.

A thunderous yell of agony froze the two heroes in shock. The sound of steel colliding with stone reverberated through the village, followed by a blood chilling howl of victory sounding from the north of the village.

"Eor Epelorn," rang out in Harthor's deep voice.

"Sounds like Harthor," murmured Zuboko, surprised to hear Harthor utter the godly command.

Instantly both he and Aerlyn were blinded by an iridescent light that spread gloriously through the alleyways and down the streets. A beam so powerful it was like a second sun. A thunderous yell of anguish drowned out the victory howl. The howl turned to a yelp and then to a whimper. The weak whimper became a last roar of pain. Aerlyn and Zuboko, now close by, witnessed a brown and black werewolf with terrible fangs, roar in agony. Its yellow, intimidating eyes were wide open in shock. Scorched hair soaked in sweat and blood with the acrid smell of burning flesh, the creature was in terrible pain, near dead and partly restored to its earthly humanoid state.

Harthor was also collapsed, armour shredded and open wounds oozing congealing blood. Although his eyes were closed and his face badly bruised and swollen, he was smiling. Pleased by his victory.

Zuboko hurriedly ran to Harthor and pulled the massacred breast plate from his semi-conscious body. A nasty shard of steel was embedded in Harthor's chest. With the breast plate now removed the wound bled freely and uncontrollably.

Harthor was a cleric, a healer, a monster killer and a religious warrior. Born to a deeply religious family he was, like his ancestors before him, a follower of the great Sun God, Epelorn. He had been schooled in swords, crossbows and had learnt the sacred spells of his chosen faith. All his weapons were enchanted, as indeed were all weapons of the Epelorn clan. His special weapon, the sword Ghamros, had been forged by his father and was responsible for the slaying of many varied beasts and demons across the plains of Dunharad.

Seven years prior, Harthor had been proclaimed the greatest cleric of the Epelorn clan, following the disappearance of the legendary cleric, Thomaz who had vanished without trace whilst journeying across the vast Richareme plains.

Harthor was strong in both body and mind and throughout the many years he had fought against evil, he had hardly ever been injured. The most pain he had ever endured had been a broken arm which he had taken as a learning experience; as a result, he had made a mental note never to underestimate an armed and dangerous skeleton!

A small crowd of townsfolk had woken from the commotion, left the safety of their beds and were now scrambling to lift the mighty bulk of Harthor to take his wounded and limp body for urgent medical attention. They did not want to lose another hero.

The next morning Harthor was still in bed. Fresh bandages smothered the seeping wounds of the night before. Calmly, nurses were feeding him medicinal potions. The badly traumatised arm that had been so savaged was wrapped and supported in a sling. Fortunately Harthor had still been out cold as the surgeon removed the shard of armour that had been embedded in his neck and repaired the laceration with sturdy sutures. His huge chest and ribcage that had been terribly crushed were healing nicely. A doctor flicked through Harthor's progress report.

"Good job Harthor is a cleric," spoke the doctor to no-one in particular, "mortal wounds, mortal wounds to any other," he continued, shaking his head.

Suddenly Harthor sat bolt upright in bed. A cold sweat smothered his short brown hair and trickled from his broad forehead, past his eyes and down to his square chin. He gasped a sharp breath and lunged for his sword that rested on the table next to his bed. One rule known to all heroes was to always have a weapon readily to hand.

"I saw the trial!" Harthor panted to Zuboko and Aerlyn. Aerlyn and Zuboko exchanged startled glances and then looked back at Harthor. Zuboko was puzzled at this sudden outburst but Aerlyn's eyes widened as the meaning of Harthor's words dawned on her. Seeing Zuboko's face, Harthor started to explain.

"First there was a path of fire, unyielding guards stood at the far end. Beyond the fire path laid a maze of changing walls with enormous spiders, the size of battle helmets, festooning the nooks and crannies. Beyond, undead souls of past soldiers directed me towards more terrible monsters." Harthor struggled for breath and guarded his smashed ribs with his one good arm.

"And…." Zuboko asked, still not understanding.

"It goes white!" Harthor drew a deep breath, closed his eyes and slept.

It was indeed the way through hell.

. Chapter Three .

THE HEALING OF HARTHOR

HARTHOR had no further outbursts and was tended well by the medics; indeed his body almost shut down as it repaired itself with the help of the magical potions. Within two days – remarkable even by the standards of the Epelorn clan - Harthor was fully healed.

Aerlyn and Zuboko had stayed close by their comrade and were both happy and relieved to see his speedy recovery. As they both entered the hut, Harthor was sat repairing his trusty sword.

"OK Harthor, now you can finally tell us what happened that night!" demanded Aerlyn, hands on hips, and keen to hear how her strong friend had become so badly injured. Aerlyn and Zuboko stared inquisitively at Harthor.

"Fine, I'll tell you," Harthor answered, sharpening his sword. He laid it carefully down in its ornate scabbard, beside the table.

That fateful night Harthor had just left Aerlyn and Zuboko in the hut and was inspecting a ravaged gnoll in vain. He could not find any clues as to the reason for the attack. Harthor had given up searching the gnoll and wandered over to an orc which had a Richareme banner embedded mortally in its throat. The orc was wearing a layer of leather straps with crude buckles as a type of protective armour. The straps were severed and its unsightly flesh dissected by an axe wound to the chest. When Harthor looked more closely at the orc, he noticed something unusual at its neck. He had never come across an orc wearing jewellery before. But there it was; a necklace in the shape of a terrible claw. Before Harthor's eyes, the skin on the insidious creature began to fade away and in its place was revealed a foul, badly scarred demon - its eyes wide open.

"What did it look like?" Zuboko asked, delving into his sack and desperately rummaging around for the ancient book he carried with him at all times. The leather bound, musty book emerged from the sack and Zuboko flicked through the pages. Each page had precise sketches of the world's demons and the collective knowledge that he had accumulated through generations of demon hunting.

"Well it looked human, only with gashes, like deep whip marks all over its body and it was surrounded and bound with chains"

The monster had quickly reared back and, taking advantage of Harthor's surprise, disappeared beyond a nearby wall. Harthor had turned instinctively at the sound of clinking chains behind him and, with quick reflexes, ducked just in time to avoid a malicious hook as the demon swung towards his head. In a reflex strike, Harthor thrust his sword deep into the creature. A green splash of ooze smeared Harthor's sword, helmet and face. The sword slashed through the demon's gut and penetrated through to its back. It appeared to have no effect. The creature piled its deadly chain into Harthor's back. Harthor responded by dragging his sword across the beast slicing off its arm. The arm fell to the ground. But, it did not remain as a severed limb. It started to claw its way in the dirt towards Harthor, long nails worming their way towards his feet. Harthor parried another flail of chains from the beast that did not seem to have even noticed that its arm had been cut clean off. As he parried, Harthor hacked at the beast's neck. The cut was not complete and the partially severed head drooped to one side remaining connected by a slither of flesh.

"Is that the best you can do?" the demon gargled, spitting at Harthor's eyes.

"I'm just getting warmed up," Harthor replied and with lightning speed and immense power he punched the monster's head off. It rolled to the ground and like the body, faded to dust.

Harthor stood poised, ready for action and breathed a heavy sign of relief when the creature did not come back to life. He had relaxed too soon. A large iron ball struck him hard across his thigh. Then he heard a snickering laugh behind him, he swung round, there it was again, to his left and right. He threw himself to the ground. Split seconds later gnarled chains whooshed overhead. Harthor turned once again to see three devilish opponents sneering at him. Harthor wasted no time. Deftly he swung his blade and sliced off the head of the nearest monster. The two remaining creatures unleashed their deadly chains directly at Harthor but with surprising agility, Harthor grabbed a chain from one devilish monster and twisted it around the neck of the other. He pulled. The neck snapped. The monsters' eyes bulged and the head, decapitated from the body, flopped to the ground. Harthor released the chain; the monster unsteadied by the release stumbled forwards. As it fell, Harthor lifted his mighty sword with both hands and the creature toppled full weight onto the razor sharp blade, immediately lopping off its head. More green goo splattered over Harthor. Harthor did not have time to be concerned as another attacker set upon him.

To his surprise, help came from a very unexpected quarter. From over the wall bounded a straggled, vicious animal. It soared through the air, muscles rippling, mouth wide open, fangs dripping with saliva. The huge mouth found its foe and bit down hard, killing the devil creature instantly.

It was a werewolf. Its snout was long and thin and it had a jaw full of jagged teeth covered in both blood and green goo. It turned and stared at Harthor with yellow emotionless eyes, every muscle and sinew in its body taut and ready to pounce. Hackles of hair ridged along the length of its supple back.

They fought. The animal leapt, slashing at Harthor with blade like claws. Harthor parried every blow. Harthor tried to take control of the battle, hacking at the lycanthrope. It was in vain; the werewolf sunk its jaws into a shoulder pad, cracking metal. Harthor struggled free, blood dripping from the puncture wounds. The sweet smell of fresh blood sent the werewolf into a frenzy. Harthor turned. It was behind him now and struck again. Harthor stumbled back, the raging beast racing at him. Harthor, scrambling in the mud, pulled a dagger from inside his shin pad and as the werewolf leapt, mouth wide to make its mortal blow, Harthor stabbed wildly upwards. The blade skewered into the werewolf's jaw.

Harthor climbed to his feet and tried to make for the protection of the wall. The werewolf, initially stunned by the attack, now swiftly followed Harthor. Harthor unhitched his crossbow from his back and hastily began to fire silver tipped arrows at the werewolf. Nothing hit.

With little effort, the beast caught Harthor and charged him down crashing the cleric to the ground and crushing his breastplate to shards. Huge claws hacked and slashed at the protective chainmail, ripping it to shreds. Blood poured from the wounds. Harthor could feel his life ebbing away and his heart rate slowing.

"For Epelorn!" he yelled in one last surge of energy.

"For Unquin!" he bellowed in rage.

"For peace!" he screamed from the pit of his soul as he crashed his blade into the werewolf. With every thrust of the blade, a silvery glow grew and grew, emanating from the very blade itself. Soon it was an immense blazing inferno. With every slash, the monster howled and drew back. Harthor and his magical sword were taking control. A leg strike caused the beast to crumple to the ground. More blows broke more bones. The beast was finished.

Harthor felt his own energy flowing away. He dropped to his knees. He saw Heaven. A white court of gardens and soft music. A throne of doves and robes of white. Pillars wrapped with red roses and Unquin sitting with Epelorn. A feast of wine and bread. A place of peace.

Harthor saw Hell. A mountain of fire and magma. There was the werewolf with Ladracsin amidst a sea of corpses, decaying and writhing with maggots. Winged rooks - devilish black vultures - swooping and grabbing at running souls. One rook found its prey and thrust its talons into the skull of a human, blood pumping freely. The human's arms and legs twitched uncontrollably as its nervous system imploded. Harthor was in Hell. He ran, sword bared. He was struck in the face. The world went white. Again.

Harthor sat up as if emerging from a deep nightmare. "That was the last thing I remember until I awoke here, covered in bandages," he concluded.

Aerlyn and Zuboko sat motionless taking in all the vivid images of the great battle Harthor had recounted.

"I've found the demon you fought!" Zuboko interrupted the silence.

"What?" Harthor questioned.

"What is it?" Aerlyn questioned suspiciously. Zuboko showed the picture in the ancient monster book to the two heroes.

"Chain-devil," Zuboko answered, "It can only be killed by decapitation!" he continued.

"This must all be linked to the attack on the village," Aerlyn murmured. It was clear she was thinking of Unquin - the bold and brave Unquin. "OK, Ladracsin has something to do with this!" Aerlyn continued.

Zuboko rummaged again, deep within his sack. After a few moments he pulled out an antiquated piece of parchment paper, tattered and torn over the passage of time.

"Behold!" exclaimed Zuboko, "a map to the mythical shrine of Ladracsin!"

. Chapter Four .

UNWELCOME VISITORS

ONCE the cries of astonishment from both Aerlyn and Harthor had subsided, Zuboko was able to explain that he had acquired the map a long time ago and had kept it secret in his safe keeping until such time as Ladracsin should rear his ugly head.

"Now seems like the right time to take it from its' wraps" offered Zuboko. "It is clear to me that Evil is abroad again and only Ladracsin can be the source of such evil"

Eager eyes poured over the map. "The best route to Ladracsin's lair is through the Kabhabab Forest and via the City of Saints – the ancient elven city, surrounded by a tropical oasis of trees and shrubs," said Zuboko in hushed tones. He had obviously spent much time studying the maps secrets.

"There we can meet with my brother, Lexon, and he will give us magical mounts to guide us past the city of Krakara and across the Medtak Dwarven Bridge toward Rakshar," added Aerlyn.

"These routes will be treacherous and Ladracsin will have left many surprises and traps; it will certainly not be an easy feat," continued Harthor.

"So be it, we will prepare this night and set off at first light," said Zuboko, looking at his comrades with pride but also trepidation.

That night, when the heroes had collected, repaired and made ready their trusty weapons they gave in to the villagers' requests to celebrate the triumph of the battle, to remember those that had not been so lucky on that fateful night and to wish the heroes a successful quest.

There was a true party atmosphere. Flags billowed in the evening breeze, music rang out, men, women and children danced, laughing merrily. Beer was served at every corner. Fat, drunken women jumped around the fires clapping in time to the rhythm. The bright, fiddling music warmed everyone's hearts.

Harthor sat on a hard, wooden bench watching Aerlyn jump elegantly between rows of benches and tables. She was throwing tiny pieces of spell crystals she had taken from Zuboko's sack. They made pink sparks that crackled and exploded as they reacted to the moisture in the air, creating an echoing barrage of sound in the night sky.

"Hey, wha's she doin'?" slurred a voice close behind Harthor. It was Zuboko. He was hiccoughing and twitching slightly. He was most certainly drunk. Harthor pulled Zuboko to a seat and as Aerlyn skipped by, he pulled her to a seat too. She too had had far too much to drink. Her eyes were glassy and she was becoming increasingly wobbly.

The mayor of the village stepped up, waving his arms dramatically towards the musicians to try to get them to pause in their playing. At last and after a few scratchy notes there was a kind of quiet.

"It is with great sadness that we send off the noble fighters and remember the tragic loss of one of their number, the great Unquin," he stated sadly. "For one of the best rangers across all Richareme fell two days ago," he added. "His tombstone will be tended daily, for, if it had not been for the bravery of these four warriors, our village would certainly have been destroyed."

As the mayor spoke and the villagers listened with compassion, something caught Harthor's keen eye. A man in black was stood on the roof of a building. His figure was difficult to make out in the night sky but as Harthor concentrated, the light from the flickering fire also showed the man was armed. The figure was aiming a crossbow directly at the Mayor. Suddenly Harthor spotted more dark figures.

"Hit the deck!" he yelled, surprising everyone. Everyone ducked or ran for cover. A guard was not quick enough and received a bolt right through his neck from point bank range.

The assassins jumped from the roofs. They were incredibly swift. But even in her drunken state, the assassins were no match for Aerlyn. One of their number lay stunned, gutted by three silver tipped arrows. Blood ran down the arrows like buttered toast. A doctor that had recently tended the heroes, tried to run. He dodged and turned, directly into the camouflaged face of an assassin. The assassin punched him, sending him headlong against a wall. A sword plunged into the doctor's chest. Moments later the assassin let out an audible groan as the point of a sword protruded from his chest wall. Zuboko had made his mark, only seconds too late to save the doctor from his bloody fate.

A guard was surrounded by the remaining assassins. The guard thrust his spear at one of his assailants, making contact and spraying blood. Two trained assassins were too much for one guard and his initial luck had now run out. They made their attack with such speed that the guard had little or no time to contemplate his end. Then, as quickly as they had descended upon the village the assassins were gone. Hiding villagers came from behind their protection and started to clear the debris and bodies.

Yet another unexplained attack! The sooner the heroes set off in search of Ladracsin the better; evil times were upon them.

. Chapter Five .

THE QUEST BEGINS

ON THE day the heroes left the village they had saved from certain massacre, hundreds of grateful villagers crowded the streets and square to say their goodbyes and their thanks. The occasion was one of mixed emotions. The heroes were pleased to see so many people but were also anxious to be setting off on such an unknown quest.

As Zuboko moved gracefully, cloak flowing behind him, small children begged him to perform some exciting magic. They danced around him, calling, laughing, pleading. Zuboko laughed back. "Fine," he called to them. He lifted his magical staff skywards and chanted. A jet of blue light soared from the staff, high into the sky and then it plummeted to the ground. It smashed onto the open ground with a resounding bang, making the children duck for cover. Zuboko laughed as the shower of purple sparks transformed into beautiful, shimmering swans that glided around the amazed children, who all cheered until the swans gradually faded away.

Aerlyn bounded forth and the crowd cheered. The people threw up the tiny flags they had been waving and immediately Aerlyn unleashed a flurry of arrows, each one making a direct hit. The crowd cheered again and applauded vigorously. A more subdued Harthor came forward; he was unusually quiet, as displays of such emotions unnerved him greatly. As a huge roar of appreciation went up, he threw forward his broad chest and raised his sword in acknowledgement.

At the rear of the crowd, four city guards dressed from head to toe in black heaved a wooden coffin past the gateway to the village. The crowd fell silent out of respect and black banners were raised. The town's guards saluted the coffin as it passed. The coffin's cargo was the body of Unquin and as a sign of respect his remains were to be burned on the hilltop just on the outskirts of the village. It had been an honourable death and it would be an honourable passing. The guards placed the coffin on the funeral pyre and nodded to Aerlyn. A solitary arrow was torched from a burning staff. Aerlyn took aim and lifted the bow towards the grey blue sky. It sailed through the air in silence, landing on and igniting the pyre. Flames engulfed the casket and dark grey smoke spiralled up high into the sky. With downcast eyes the heroes turned and made their first steps to rid the world of Ladracsin's evil.

. Chapter Six .

THOMAZ

SEVEN years previously......

Thomaz was surrounded. A sea of hobgoblins, chain devils and vampires lay before him, all jeering hungrily at the cleric. Thomaz did not flinch. Arrogantly he combed a wooden stake through his lank hair, made ready his giant spear and calmly said, "Well, you are slightly out numbered!" They all swarmed in on him!

The ugly beasts thought Thomaz to be easy prey and would make a fine supper but Thomaz had very different ideas as the first of the beasts to reach the prey soon discovered to their cost. Immediately a hobgoblin was speared through the neck. With a reverse thrust a vampire was staked by the spear's sharpened handle. Immediately it turned to dust. In the melee, there was a flurry of metal, blood, skin and dust. None of it belonged to Thomaz. Monsters were being torn apart. The battle was over in minutes and the beasts massacred.

"Well, that was nice, pity it's all over!" Thomaz purred charmingly to himself.

"OHRU, TIKA, MALU SHUKA," boomed a voice from in the shadows, directly behind Thomaz. He turned abruptly but saw nothing although he had a strange sense that he recognised the commanding voice. In response to the strange tongue - and to Thomaz's disappointment - the demons that he had minutes ago destroyed were rising from the dead. Thomaz drew in a deep breath and braced himself for more action.

"Great! More fun!" Thomaz sighed sarcastically.

As Thomaz launched a spear through the neck of a chain devil, he saw to his surprise his gnollish friend Rugtak charge through an archway into the hall, armed with a pike. Enemy reinforcements piled in. Orc archers fired at Thomaz, who was caught in a brutal melee. Two goblin heads smashed together as Thomaz remorselessly brought his spear crashing down.

Rugtak was now at a standstill, completely surrounded by marauding demons. His sturdy pike was ripped from his strong hands just as an axe was swung towards his chest. Blood sprayed the grey, stone floor. Rugtak, fallen, lay in a pool of blood. A fearsome scimitar was raised high into the air.

On the other side of the great hall, a head rolled. Thomaz had remembered the owner of the commanding voice that had summoned these ferocious demons back from the dead and when the druid had stepped from the shadows into the light, he had been ready. Thomaz launched his attack and the druid's head rolled across the floor. Instantly the remaining demons crashed to the ground as the magic used to reanimate them was destroyed by the death of the druid. Thomaz looked around at the carnage. His eyes fell on the body of Rugtak, lying still and cold in the dust. Thomaz's final attack had come too late for Rugtak.

"Pity," murmured Thomaz, coolly and without an ounce of compassion.

As Thomaz turned his gaze from the massacre, the room became illuminated by the glow of fiery sprites that whooshed across the hall, moulding through statues and stone and collecting over the body of Rugtak. Within seconds the bright glow was absorbed by Rugtak's body, which started to twitch and jabber barely audibly, "Door...Kill....Lava.... Doorkilllava!"

Rugtak's corpse started to glow red hot and dissolved into a steaming liquid. With a life of its own, the liquid started to divide and separate into vast numbers of similar sized pools.

Simultaneously the liquid pools started to rise up and take on the form of lava beasts all identical to one another, moving together, and all in the direction of Thomaz. They all advanced. Thomaz had never encountered these creatures before and was undecided upon what action to take. Brute force took over and Thomaz sliced one of the lava troopers. It formed into two creatures that continued to advance for an attack.

"That has made things a little more difficult," said Thomaz, starting to become a little concerned for his welfare as the beasts loomed closer. It was rare for Thomaz to resort to his final choice of action but needs must. He turned and ran. He ran through an ornate archway, scrambled through a circular grating and into a sewer. He splashed through the foul smelling water and at a junction climbed a stairway which took him higher and higher up into a tower. There appeared to be no escape, the creatures were relentless and were now surrounding him. He was trapped in the tower. One of the creatures, gibbering insanely, was within slicing distance and through frustration Thomaz did not hesitate, crashing his spear through the molten liquid. The liquid formed into two new forms and continued to move towards Thomaz. In his frustration Thomaz yelled at the creatures," Where is Rugtak?"

In garbled tones all the fiends responded to the question at the same time, "Me!" was their answer.

"There is no Rugtak, he is dead. You are foul demons!" Thomaz screamed back. "Which one of you is the source, who do I need to kill to stop you?"

Immediately the gibbering and forward momentum of the lava beasts stopped and they remained motionless. Thomaz looked at the creatures in bewilderment as the searing heat from their red hot masses scorched the hairs on his skin.

The red hot mass closest to Thomaz, now coherent, spoke calmly and sensibly, "Alas, my pathetic friend, I am an upper being!" the voice boomed, resounding from the walls of the tower. "I do not die, I do not feel pity. I have the collective mind and memory of every being transformed into a higher being! You too will be destroyed and added to our collected entities."

Thomaz's mind was racing, how was he going to escape this? He had vague recollections from his childhood of tales of these higher beings. He remembered the nights around the fires as the elders retold legends which were then passed from generation to generation. He remembered that these higher beings were capable of shape shifting and taking on the identity of any of the species added to their collective will.

The higher beings again moved forwards toward Thomaz to absorb his identity and knowledge. Thomaz's fighting instincts came to the fore, as he had no desire to be part of anything. He roared, "I may not kill you but I will go down trying!"

The higher beings transformed again and became massive molten cobras, coiled and poised to strike with glowing fangs. In unison, the cobra heads darted forwards, plunging their penetrating fangs into Thomaz's body, easily puncturing the skin. Thomaz prepared himself for death. Somehow he had not imagined it would end so abruptly. Suddenly to Thomaz's surprise and absolute relief the cobras started to shrivel and wither to the floor.

"Vampire," they screamed out in unison, writhing and shape shifting from one species to another uncontrollably.

"Half vampire actually!" Thomaz responded arrogantly, laughing with relief that his luck had lasted and that what he had thought would be his mortal enemy were now meeting their doom.

Thomaz, with increasing confidence turned to face the rest of the beings and smiled slowly. Unused to this attack of force, the creatures were powerless and were only able to try to make an escape. With only the slightest movement of his narrow lips, Thomaz recited an ancient spell. His eyes turned the darkest of black, edged with a glow of raging fire. A spell of speed! It propelled him forwards and now he was in front of the fleeing beings.

Thomaz knew that the creatures were easily able to shape shift but he did not know that they were also able to blend and form an actual single entity. As they came closer to Thomaz the multiple beasts melted and combined to form a ten foot tall, muscular, horned terror rampaging its way toward him at full speed.

The blood red creature's slick body was covered in a thick red slime. Jagged horns protruded from its bulbous forehead. In its pulsating fist, it carried a nightmarish, wrought iron broad sword. It rammed its bulging chest at Thomaz and knocked him cart wheeling into a dusty wall, sending hairy spiders scuttling for the cover of dark corners.

Thomaz picked himself up from the rubble, "Well that has made things interesting!" he groaned. Thomaz hurled his spear at the great beast. It snapped like a toothpick, raining splinters onto the stone, cobbled floor. The hulking foe had not even been scratched. "Okay! That hasn't made things easier!" Thomaz moaned sarcastically. He pulled out his trusty weapon, a long, narrow stake.

The fiend bellowed a terrifying war cry as it crashed at Thomaz again. This time its malevolent sword dug deep into the flesh of Thomaz's shoulder. Blood gushed forth like an erupting volcano. The pain was unbearable but Thomaz relentlessly gouged at the beast's horned temple. The creature opened its gaping mouth wide to reveal a worm like tongue. The tongue unravelled and then entwined itself around Thomaz's neck and started to tighten, making Thomaz's jugular engorge and pulsate in a vain attempt to drag in oxygen. Thomaz struggled to lift up his arm, his hand still clinging desperately to the wooden stake. He plunged the stake into the tightening flesh of the tongue. The impaled tongue released its grip on Thomaz's throat and whipped back and forth in a frenzy.

As the tongue lashed about uncontrollably, it became smeared with the blood that was still seeping from the wound on Thomaz's shoulder. The writhing of the tongue grew more and more intense as the creature absorbed the half vampire's blood to hasten its own doom. It jerked, thrashed and shrivelled, finally collapsing in a burst of red flames and screaming the agonising accusation, "KILLER! Killer of an entire race!"

"Oh yeah!" jeered Thomaz arrogantly. "Yeah, I guess I am," he added casually. It had been a tough challenge and more than once Thomaz had feared that this would be his last day on this mortal plain. As he stood and watched, the embers of his foe - white luminescent spirits - floated in spirals up into the sky. Up to Heaven. Entrancing and magical. Spellbound, Thomaz gazed as they made their final journey. Released from their captives, the collective entity, they took on their earthly forms; their individual forms. Thomaz could make out one spirit with wolf like features. He stood tall and proud and raised his sword in salute to his mighty companion, Rugtak.

"Hail, Rugtak, greatest gnoll in history!" Thomaz yelled nobly. The spirit rose higher and higher. His battling companion had risen to a higher plain. Thomaz, weary and hardened by thirty years of casual death, nonetheless shed a solitary tear at the passing of Rugtak.

Thomaz had only seconds of reprieve as he started at the sound of loud, slow clapping from behind him. He swivelled, weapon poised to kill whoever was foolish enough to be taunting him. He could see nothing there other than the humongous corpse.

"Very impressive! Moments after you weep over death, you are ready for more of the same! Very impressive!" a spine chilling voice echoed around the room, making the hackles stand erect on Thomaz's neck. "I see you need a new weapon!" the voice resounded. "Here take my sword, I will not need it!"

Suddenly, and startling the poised Thomaz, a large coal black broadsword clattered to the dust ridden floor. A dragons head was lodged at the handle like a battle decoration. Runes embellished the handle like a wand. Thomaz's mind started to race.

"Well, I do need a new weapon and it is bound to be a rough journey home!" Thomaz mused to himself trying to justify the need for such a weapon. A weapon freely given by a stranger. Thomaz was hypnotised by the ornate sword and wanted it for his own. Against his own better judgement, Thomaz stooped forward and stretched out his blood smeared hand to grasp the rune decorated handle. As his fingers closed around the shaft, his heart bounded with the excitement at possessing the gift.

He lifted the blade and the fading light glinted on the silver, razor sharp blade. Instantly Thomaz let out a wail of anguish. The hardy leather and metal armour Thomaz was wearing started to weld itself to his muscular frame. The searing pain ripped through the whole of his body. The supple leather transformed into dark, scaled purple chain mail. Screaming in pain, Thomaz fell forward onto his knees and two nodular growths ripped forth from his spine, growing until they formed solid batwings that beat and flapped at their formation. He threw back his head and bellowed as reddish horns erupted from the flesh of his rugged, handsome face. Enormous fangs protruded from his jaw and his skin became a layer of black thorns. All human likeness had vanished. The wails of terror stopped and there in the evening shadows stood the devilish form of a vampire. A true blood vampire!

"Welcome!" boomed the voice once again, "The dark side has arisen. Thomaz is gone! You are a true blood!"

A ripple of pleasure ran up the nodular spine of the vampire and an overwhelming desire to feed throbbed in every cell of its transformed body. It uncurled its massive, leathery wings and soared off into the night sky.

With its immense speed and heightened senses, it did not take long for the vampire to search out fresh flesh to dine upon. Streaking through the darkness under the glittering stars the vampire circled and assessed its prey.

There appeared to be a troll training camp down below. Monstrous, seven foot tall ogres towered above their goblin adversaries. Groups fought hand to hand combat, while others trained with gruesome and barbaric weapons.

The vampire circled again, folded back its great wings and soared for the attack on the unsuspecting beasts that were already exhausted and weary from training. One monstrosity swung a rusted axe at a smaller, purple demon. The smaller warrior stood its ground as the axe crashed into him and shattered into shards of metal which clattered to the ground. Within seconds the axe wielding creature reeled backwards. The vampire was on his back and with one swift action sunk its black razor fangs into the beast's neck and fed.

Green gunge seeped like honey from the punctured neck. Simultaneously, a claw gorged through to the ogre's spinal cord pulling out fragments of bone. The creature's body fell forwards, jerking limply and crashing down with an ominous crack. The vampire dislodged its deadly fangs and with one swift movement ripped off the head and hurled it at a wall where it splattered like a paint effect.

Individual battles stopped and all eyes turned to the gloating vampire as it stood at full height satisfied from such a hearty feed. The vampire licked its fangs and wiped the blood drools away with its arm and looked at the other tasty morsels before it.

"Feed! Feed on them all!" boomed the terrible voice.

"With pleasure!" responded the Vampire and with a flurry of wings and a frenzy of fangs, the feeding massacre commenced. Within minutes there were monster body parts strewn everywhere with the vampire at the centre of the devastation, sucking the final juices from the torn organs with relish. The vampire beast was a formidable killing machine.

Over the next seven years, the vampire, who had taken the much feared name Thomz, from some long distant memory of its previous existence, was supported and encouraged by the ever watching and ever present resounding voice as it plundered the lands. Many lands - human and demonic - had fallen and now lived under the rule of the booming voice and the fear of the deadly vampire.

Only Richareme had managed to avoid being taken, although often its borders had been breached.

"Very good vampire!" congratulated the voice.

"I told you to call me Thomz," snarled the vampire.

Thomz was stood at the base of a mountain on the coast of Edron and awaited his master's instruction.

"Do not go into Richareme," commanded the voice.

"Why?" Thomz interrogated.

"Word spreads of heroes at the edge of Richareme; we send orcs in first and save you for the grand finale!" the voice whispered maliciously.

"Much easier kills," Thomz sneered, "Just women and children," he sighed as though he was in paradise. "Deal!" he gibed happily.

The voice had therefore had Thomz dispatch an army of orcs to deal with these heroes. Things had not, however, gone to plan and within days the remnants of the army returned, their numbers vastly depleted and those left badly injured. Thomz was enraged. The leading orc officer had given a full battle report to the voice which informed him of their great defeat and the cowardly way they had departed the battle ground, having killed only one hero.

"Worthless orcs! A worthless army!" Thomz scorned.

The voice too was mortified by their defeat. "Kill them, kill them all!"

Thomz needed no further encouragement and was pleased to dish out a malicious punishment to the orcs for their failure.

He was like a raging tiger attacking its prey. Terrified orcs ran as best as their injuries allowed them, but to no avail. Thomz was so fast it was difficult to see him with the naked eye. Only the devastation and destruction that he left behind marked his path. Decapitated heads rolled, guts spewed as talons and teeth flashed. Soon the grass was stained with the blood and the gruesome corpses of the eviscerated army. Which was now no more. The massacre was horrifically brief. Not a single survivor.

"Useless orcs, they failed completely. The only compensation is their slaying of one hero!" the voice rasped venomously.

"It was fortunate that we also sent the werewolf and those loathsome chain devils!" grumbled Thomz.

At that moment, however, through the debris of decomposing corpses came a solitary chain devil, head bowed low and fearing instant death from its masters; Thomz and the voice. It dropped to its knees before Thomz, chains clanging as they clashed together with every cumbersome movement.

"Gorshang the werewolf is dead, my masters!" the creature uttered, head still bowed. Its fear had not been without good reason as its head was dissected from its body in one clean slash of Thomz's sword as he raged against this incompetent.

"What now, master?" Thomz growled angrily at the voice.

"A change of plan is needed, I think. Let us start to divide and weaken this land. There is a city in Richareme ruled by ancient elf half breeds" the voice instructed. "It must be destroyed before I lead my mighty army out from Rakshar and unleash the full terror of our forces upon the world. Go yourself, take an army and raze it to the ground! Bring me the body of the elf lord, Lexon!" it ordered.

Thomz turned and left the rubble and carnage at his feet and started on the long journey to obey – as always - his master's wishes.

. Chapter Seven .

A WEB OF SHADOWS

HARTHOR was exhausted. The heroes had been travelling for a long time and were now trying to make their way through Kakhabab Forest. Kakhabab Forest was notoriously impassable and Harthor's huge bulk made things even more difficult. He was exhausted and becoming angrier and angrier as he was incessantly scratched by whipping branches and bitten by irritating tiny insects that seemed to find Harthor particularly tasty. He was also collecting unwanted pieces of plant camouflage that caught between his armour plates and slowed his progress further by tangling onto other branches and shrubs. Aerlyn smiled to herself as Harthor grumbled and huffed behind her. She was lithe and agile and the dense overgrowth caused her little concern. Aerlyn's natural instincts for woodland survival came to the fore and she was in her element as she elegantly leapt and bounded over branches and the tangled undergrowth. Zuboko was not suffering the conditions of the forest either and had used his druid powers to make the barbs and branches bend and flex leaving room for him to pass.

The light was fading fast. Even more quickly now as they moved further into the canopy of the vast forest. Every tree looked similar and it was easy to become disorientated and lost. It was fortunate that they were able to see by the beams of light shooting from Zuboko's staff. As their eyes focused in the changing light, they became uncomfortably aware of hundreds, maybe thousands, of glass-like glowing beads in the cover of the thick undergrowth.

"What do you think that is?" Harthor piped up, trying to make conversation in a desperate attempt to distract his mind from the growing amount of foliage his armour was picking up as he made his way through the ever thickening tangle of plants.

"I don't care. I don't think we should allow ourselves to become distracted, it could be an ambush!" said Aerlyn in hushed but stern tones. Aerlyn tried to keep her voice calm but her anxiety was growing. She had heard the folk tales about the great forest and was keen that they maintained their speed and did not fall prey to the inhabitants of the forest.

In a flurry of legs, they were set upon. Tarantulas swarmed from the branches. Thick, hairy legs carried bulbous bodies scuttling at the heroes. Others unravelled long, fine threads and hung precariously in the air suspended from the highest branches. All were hungry and fangs drooled with saliva and venom in anticipation of devouring their prey.

These creatures were enormous, man sized! Harthor was knocked to the ground instantly by the attack of a massive brown and black, mottled fiend. With a jet of sparks, Zuboko blasted the beast from Harthor's back. On impact, it froze to a solid ball of ice. The winded Harthor nodded his thanks to his comrade as he scrambled to his feet, perpetually slowed by the multitude of brambles and twigs that adorned his armour.

Aerlyn swiftly climbed the nearest pine tree, dodging spiders as she sprang up. She pulled a dagger from the shinguard at her ankle and sliced through the fine, glistening threads. Suspended arachnids plummeted to their doom. Aerlyn closed her eyes at the overwhelming brightness of an exploding purple star conjured by the mighty Zuboko. It struck the swarm like a meteor. Many died on impact and the remainder, fearing the intense bright light, scuttled a hasty retreat back into the blackness of the forest. Aerlyn gracefully back flipped from her position high in the tree, landing next to an ominous black widow that was poised ready to strike a deadly bite. Without hesitation, Aerlyn sliced her bowstring across the creature's neck, splashing spider juice. It fell limp immediately.

Harthor had been greatly disadvantaged during the attack. His great size prevented him from swinging his sword with any accuracy. It had sliced into many of the bushes and trees that cramped him. Harthor lashed at a retreating spider. Unfortunately his sword lodged into a mossy stump. He heaved but could not remove the weapon. The spider sensing Harthor's disadvantage turned and launched a poisonous assault. Forced to defend, Harthor stopped his struggle to release the sword and grappled for his shield. Luck was with the mighty warrior and the immense shield crashed into the advancing spider smashing it to a pulp.

Previously concentrated on their individual battles for survival, Aerlyn and Harthor became aware that Zuboko was struggling to defeat his adversary. Zuboko had dropped his magical staff during the conflict and a grotesque spider was now on top of him and trying to sink its venomous fangs into Zuboko's flesh. "Guys... a little hand here...!" Zuboko called desperately.

Harthor immediately stepped forward to assist Zuboko but as he stooped under a gnarled and twisted branch, his progress was abruptly halted as he was assaulted by a ferocious Dengous spider, a skeletal wolf breed. The creature was notoriously cunning and difficult to defeat. It reared up its two front bony, legs instantly doubling its size, while long octopus-like tendrils thrashed and tried to stifle its prey. The beast glared at Harthor with all eight of its beady, yellow eyes. The crashing of its strong mandible exposed intermittently the razor sharp fangs. Harthor was in a cramped and compromised position. The Dengous spider moved closer ready to kill.

Aerlyn who had also heard Zuboko's call for help saw that Harthor's need was greater. With a mighty leap from her slender legs, she soared into the sky slashing with all her strength at the twisting tendrils. Her sharp blade sliced. The spider reared again. Aerlyn leapt again just in time to avoid one of the black tendrils which darted at her leg. Again she sliced with the blade and again the tendrils were severed. The spider screeched and thrashed its strong mandible, rearing up to lurch violently at Harthor. The vast fangs made contact and the huge beast bit down. Harthor's reinforced chain mail armour saved him again. The beast withdrew from the attack and reared again to thrust at any exposed flesh. Aerlyn, still fighting majestically, had by now ripped a poison laden fang from the dead black widow that lay slumped in the overgrowth. Another mighty leap and Aerlyn landed square on the back of the Dengous spider. She steadied herself, raised her arm and with all her might plunged the deadly fang into the skull of Harthor's attacker. The spider reared one final time and screeched as the poison seared through its demonic body. The yellow eyes rolled and bulged as the spider fought for survival. With the snapping of bone, the beast crumbled to the ground, all life force gone.

Both the heroes turned their attention back towards Zuboko who, much to his own relief, had managed to scramble to his staff which he was now busy running through the creature that had come so close to sinking its deadly fangs into him. Dark, syrup like blood oozed from the impaled spider's abdomen and trickled down the staff. Harthor and Aerlyn simultaneously shouted a warning to Zuboko, who was now trying to remove the sticky staff from the creature's body, but it came too late and another spider piled into the back of the unsuspecting shaman, who was sent sprawling to the floor yet again. Zuboko flinched and groaned as the beast sank its huge fangs into his leg and pumped him with deadly venom. Zuboko slumped to the ground as the poison tracked its way mercilessly through his blood vessels seeking out the vital organs in an attempt to extinguish his life. In fury, Harthor launched his heavy shield at the Behemoth spider, breaking the creature's exoskeleton with a resounding crack. The fangs released from Zuboko's leg and the crushed beast lay on the ground next to its victim.

The poison was taking effect and Zuboko was losing consciousness. The two heroes dropped to their knees at his side and Aerlyn cradled his disfigured head. Zuboko was moaning but it was barely audible. Aerlyn put her tiny ear near to his mouth and tried to understand what Zuboko was trying to say.

"Snow herb!" Zuboko whispered with what was sure to be one of his last breaths. Aerlyn grabbed for Zuboko's sack and tipped its contents onto the grass.

"What...?" Harthor started to ask.

"SNOW HERB! We must find snow herb!" answered Aerlyn even before Harthor could ask the question.

They both frantically rummaged through the leather draw string pouches that carried the magical herbs and read the labels in ornate script on the tiny bottles of potions.

"HERE!" called Harthor. He was holding a small pouch, tied with a gold and red cord. Aerlyn released the cord and tipped the contents onto her smooth palm.

"What now?" Harthor asked. "Does he have to eat it?"

"Zuboko, ZUBOKO!" said Aerlyn, patting his cheek to rouse him. "Zuboko, what do we do now? We have the snow herb!"

Zuboko's eyes flickered weakly and he mumbled vague instructions. Immediately, Aerlyn thrust a large clump of the herb into her mouth and began to chew vigorously. Harthor followed suit. Soon, green drool dripped from their mouths. Aerlyn spat out the bitter tasting pulp and started to smear it on the wound. Again Harthor copied Aerlyn's actions. The juice was immediately absorbed into the puncture marks and traced the path previously taken by the venom. As they held their breath, colour started to gradually reappear in Zuboko's features; the snow herb had destroyed the active compound and saved Zuboko.

Zuboko opened his eyes and saw the concerned faces of his fellow heroes who smiled with relief as they saw his strength returning. Zuboko struggled to his feet and thrust forth his mighty staff.

"By the Lords Epelorn and Semandur, I send these devils' lackeys back to hell!" thundered Zuboko.

The creatures' screeches echoed through the forest like the sound of a hundred crazed banshees. Aerlyn and Harthor clasped their hands to their ears in a vain effort to blot out the excruciating sound. Zuboko stood tall, staff raised, as vibrating rings of energy pulsed from the mighty staff. From the chaos of the writhing spiders rose the torso of a grotesque, hair-covered demon and made its way, apparently unaffected by the pulsating energy surging from the staff, towards Zuboko. Huge ribs jutted from its barrel chest stretching its hairy skin and protruding into long, multi-jointed legs. The demon's head had been slashed and now appeared as red and raw as a poorly healed scar. Eight beady black eyes surrounded a pug nose at the centre of its face. It advanced on Zuboko, wielding a rusted axe, twisting and turning the shaft, spinning the menacing blade through the air like a crazed juggler. Harthor and Aerlyn watched as the creature moved closer and closer to Zuboko unperturbed by Zuboko's magic. Neither of the heroes had weapons ready at hand. Harthor looked around frantically for a makeshift weapon. Frustrated, he grasped at a branch. He threw the branch. It hit the beast right in the middle of the beady black eyes.

"A twig! You're going to kill it with a twig?" Aerlyn moaned sarcastically as the beast came into slicing distance of Zuboko.

The fiendish monster stopped dead in its tracks and crashed backwards to the ground, dead. Aerlyn's jaw dropped open and her eyes became bright and round in amazement.

"Amazing what you can do with a bit of wood!" Zuboko piped up as he lowered his staff and the terrible, pulsating sound disappeared into the leaves and branches of the forest, leaving an eerie quietness.

With their leader dead, the remaining spawn of spiders fled into the darkness, in terror, without trace. Aerlyn strode to a nearby spider corpse, a mutilated tarantula, and ripped an embedded bolt from one of its many legs. The bolt dripped green slime.

"Typical! Whenever you destroy spiders you can bet that you will always ruin your best arrows with bug juice!" Aerlyn complained uncharacteristically.

Harthor too looked for his abandoned weapons. It was an unpleasant task and all three heroes were dismayed at how much bug slime now covered them. A multitude of biting insects had gathered over the decomposing bodies of the fallen spiders. It was time for the heroes to move on. As they braced themselves for the hard slog through the forest, Zuboko noticed a rune on the spider leader's chest. He bent forward to examine it.

It was not a large rune and it was only thanks to the keen eyes of the shaman that this lucky discovery had been made. The rune was decorated with a cryptic trident. Zuboko pulled a small blade from his side and sliced through the leather cording that suspended the rune from the leader's thick, hairy neck. Harthor and Aerlyn caught up to Zuboko and stooped down to examine Zuboko's discovery.

"It is the symbol for 9 in Ladracsin's runes!" exclaimed Harthor.

Zuboko fingered the symbol and turned the rune. Embossed on the reverse side was a bat wing emblem. "That is the cult sign of Shiargh!" gasped Aerlyn.

Harthor was all too familiar with the cult of Shiargh and was already responsible for terminating two of its ever reducing members, the werewolf and a zombie. He had now helped in the destruction of a third; the spider leader. Shiargh was notorious for its evil acts throughout the lands lead by the infamous Ladracsin and the terrifying un-named demon that travelled from region to region carrying out the evil intents of its master. It was only known as the Death Bringer.

"So, Shiargh are involved. Just as we suspected, Ladracsin!" Harthor concluded.

"We'd better get moving!" muttered Aerlyn. "If we haven't become too lost, the City of Saints is not too much further!"

. Chapter Eight .

BESIEGED

LEXON'S fiery, elven blade sliced through the hobgoblin's exposed chest. A thin line of crimson blood splashed the elf's protective breastplate. The main parapets of the City of Saints were being overrun.

"Lexon, Lexon!" someone bellowed at Lexon's side. Lexon turned and saw a lone soldier racing to do battle with a huddle of four orcs and a dashing, dark elf. The soldier thrust a rapier towards the chest of the dark elf. Its deadly point sliced deep into his flesh. As the lone soldier withdrew the blade, he agilely kicked out his slender leg at an orc and sent it spinning off the wall and crashing to the ground.

A second later, Lexon stood at the soldier's side. With immense strength and speed, Lexon slashed his mighty sword at the remaining two orcs. As their rivals drew their last breaths, the two warriors turned to face each other and smiled. The two had battled alongside one another on many occasions and were firm friends. Just as Lexon had raised his muscular arm to clap his companion on the arm, the expression on the soldier's face changed. No longer were the eyes smiling at Lexon, they had suddenly shadowed in first shock and then fear. A trickle of blood crept from the edge of his now grimacing lips and he clasped his hands to his stomach, doubling over in pain. The wooden shaft of a crossbar bolt protruded from his abdomen.

"No!" cried out Lexon. Lexon caught his companion as he slowly dropped to the ground, his face ashen. Lexon cradled his head as the warrior struggled to take his last precious breaths. The soldier's head lolled to one side and his eyes became fixed. Gently, Lexon passed his mudded hand over the soldier's eyes and they closed in eternal sleep. Saint Maine had fought his last battle and now, rested in peace. Lexon lifted his face to the sky and roared. Leaping to his feet, adrenaline pumping through his veins, Lexon jumped down the steps, thrusting, hacking and slashing at all adversaries in his path to reach the crossbow sniper and take revenge for his comrade's death.

More and more orcs poured onto the stairway making the route to the sniper arduous and slow. Lexon could see the sniper tucked away and taking aim at his next victim; frustrated, he looked on as the sniper unleashed a bolt. The bolt soared through the air, silent and deadly. Lexon followed its path only to realise to his dismay it was in direct line towards a swirling green cape. Parlavor! The bolt hit its target directly between the shoulder blades. On impact, the cloaked elf threw out his arms and fell forwards onto the driving blade of an attacking orc. Lexon looked on, shocked. The elf, Saint Parlavor, had fallen.

Lexon parried more orc attacks as his eyes scanned the fighting hordes for the blue cloak of Saint Eldered. To his dismay, his attention was caught by the movement of a bloodied blue cloak and a swinging blade. Saint Eldered was battling against overwhelming odds and there was no way for Lexon to break through to help. Dismayed, Lexon watched on as Saint Eldered became overpowered by the massive, attacking force and stumbled to the ground only to be impaled by a multitude of blades. Lexon looked away in horror.

With renewed energy and rage, Lexon lunged forwards, hacking at his startled adversaries and slicing their limbs into worthless strips. He climbed onwards over the increasing mound of severed bodies. His clothes and body completely saturated with the blood of his foes. When would this evil end?

This day he already had seen his brothers and closest friends die. All bar one. Aerlyn. Brave Aerlyn, who had left the City of Saints for the lands ofR

ichareme in the company of a trio of heroes fighting the evils that were spreading through the lands. She was all that was left that was dear to him and he vowed there and then that he would survive this battle and ensure that Aerlyn did not meet the same fate as his brothers. Before the start of this mighty massacre, Lexon had just had news of the heroes and of the passing of Unquin. As his mind conjured pictures of his sister, he routinely took a strike at an advancing orc whose arms were raised high, ready to bring down a double handed broad sword. The orc's arms fell to the ground taking the broad sword with them.

As Lexon fought for his life, he feared that Ladracsin's evil had finally arrived at the City of Saints and that all would be lost to the realms of darkness and despair on this day. The strength was starting to seep from his body. Everything was becoming desolate. All hope was lost!

Suddenly, a distraction from behind. Lexon whirled round to witness a mob of attacking orcs being blown through the air by the rays of a crimson explosion of seismic proportions. A cataclysmic great sword hacked across the rear of their force like a frenzied troll hungry for death and pain.

"Hello Lexon, brother dear!" called Aerlyn sweetly.

A gang of orcs turned at the sound of her call and ran directly at her, cackling an angry war cry. All fell, impaled by a flurry of arrows.

"Feel the wrath of the Gods!" Harthor roared, raising his arm towards the grey, cloudy sky. Flames erupted from the air blasting his opponents and melting them into one hot, molten mass.

In one swift swoop, Zuboko struck his weapon into the ribcage of a bewildered hobgoblin. It penetrated deep and erupted from the beasts back. With another sharp movement and twist, Zuboko pulled and a secondary adversary was mortally wounded.

Revitalised by the presence of the heroes, Lexon unleashed the last of his energy and rage. With his trusty blade, he lunged at the neck of a goblin and slit it from ear to ear. The goblin gurgled, dropping to his knees, spewing vast amounts of viscous blood. A grim smile came to Lexon's lips; perhaps now, all was not lost. Maybe there was a chance! Just as the thought of victory entered his mind he was grabbed from behind by the arm by a strong and grotesque troll. He heard a snap and then fell back doubling in agony. The troll, sensing an easy kill, loomed over Lexon. Lexon, ashen white with pain, braced himself for the mortal blow. Aerlyn, protective of her brother, leaped between the troll and Lexon.

"Get away from him, you scum!" she bellowed. She raised her bow and sent a frenzy of arrows directly at the heart of the gruesome beast. All made their mark and the troll crashed to the ground narrowly missing both Aerlyn and Lexon. Immediately, another beast replaced the troll and thrust its rusted weapon dangerously close to Aerlyn. Fortunately, with immense grace she was able to dodge the blow and another battle to the death began.

Harthor fired a rugged crossbow that he had retrieved from the body of one of their enemy. The bolt hit a pug-nosed goblin and the impact knocked him to the ground, squealing in pain. Harthor swiftly turned and rammed his celestial sword into a midget goblin. It gurgled and spat blood and crashed onto the impressive body pile.

Zuboko ran to Harthor, "We can't hold them for much longer!" he insisted as he frantically torched the fiend that was battling him.

"I know!" Harthor panted as he slammed a studded fist into a troll's hooked nose, smashing the bones on impact and causing a cascade of blood to pump from its remains.

During the skirmish, Lexon had passed out in pain and weariness. A golden crested dark elf strode out towards his limp body and with great strength for his size lifted him over his shoulder and made his way for the cover of a ruined wall.

As he was about to reach the cover of the wall he froze then fell forwards as a gold encrusted arrow pierced his back and penetrated through the other side and out of his chest. A trickle of blood soaked around the golden tipped arrow. Aerlyn's shot was true; she had come to her brothers' rescue again.

Aerlyn nimbly darted over the bodies that littered the ground towards her brother's body. Was he still alive? Quickly, she felt for the pulse at his neck, it was weak but still there. She mustered all her strength and lifted his motionless body and staggered towards the safety of the keep.

Zuboko and Harthor had already made their way to the keep and were deep in battle, holding off a battalion of dark elves. Aerlyn slumped to her knees, breathing heavily at the massive exertion. As gently as possible, she lowered Lexon to the keep's floor that was smeared with blood and strewn with bodies. As she rested his head on an abandoned shield, her eyes were drawn to a body that she recognised. She recalled the long grey hair and the aged but sharp features of the face of her father. He was still and cold to the touch. The shaft of a long spear protruded from his sturdy and ornate chest armour. Aerlyn was wracked with a flood of emotions; shock, sadness, fear and then anger.

She rounded to where Harthor and Zuboko were holding off the dark elves and unleashed the boundless anger that was surging through her body.

"You killed my friend!" she shrieked, eyes blazing, and shot one of the dark elves down.

"You killed my father!" She cried, whilst impaling a hobgoblin with a flurry of arrows.

"Now I will kill YOU!" she screamed and tore apart the forces trying to enter the keep. Arrows screeched through the stagnant air taking down her foes on impact. These dark elves were no match for the enraged Aerlyn who by now was moving at such speed, her actions were blurs without true definition.

Zuboko, exhausted by his battles, was relieved to take a step back and regain his breath as he watched his two comrades cutting through the ranks of the enemy. Both spurred on by their overwhelming emotions. One for vengeance and the other for the greater good.

Harthor's sword was slicing so fast it was burning and as the heat and flames made contact with the green slime-like blood the smell became putrid and the flames turned an intense green.

The body piles were becoming larger and larger but still the enemy came, hoping that their attack would be the one that counted against these mighty heroes, but still Aerlyn and Harthor battled on with no sense of exhaustion. The ranks of attacking dark elves had all become deceased and only orcs entered the death filled keep. The swarm of orcs, realising that their attempts to defeat the heroes were futile, fled, clearing from the ruined city and heading for the safety of the forest.

As the fighting subsided, Zuboko exited the keep relieved to breathe fresh air and to try to remove the foul stench of death and burning flesh from his nostrils. As he coughed and spat the foul taste from his mouth, he saw one single demon stood on a pile of lifeless bodies. It was the dark elf, his dark armour elegantly trimmed with gold, that had tried to take the body of Lexon.

"Who are you?" Zuboko stuttered as he drew his staff forward ready to attack.

"Your slayer!" he screeched as he drew his spear.

The dark elf held out his left arm and gestured to the heroes, beckoning them to make the first move. Harthor charged. Aerlyn fired a flurry of arrows and Zuboko cast a fiery red flame from his staff. The arrows arrived first. The dark elf made a swing with his spear at the incoming arrows and smashed them into harmless wooden shards that simply scattered at his feet. Then, as though in slow motion and as limber as a gymnast, he arched his back and the force of the flaming inferno missed its target and crashed into a once sturdy wall sending rocks and boulders soaring in all directions in a massive explosion. Harthor was thundering down the embankment gathering speed and strength for an almighty attack only for the dark elf to perform the same slow motion movement and easily dodge the attack. As Harthor's enormous bulk passed, forced forwards by his momentum, the dark elf lunged his spear at Harthor, impaling his forearm. The spear tore through his flesh as Harthor's forward momentum ripped the sharp steel along and out.

Anger clouded Zuboko's judgement and he rushed in to defend his comrade. "I will avenge you! My friend!" he roared as he plummeted down the embankment, sword and staff raised for the kill.

Zuboko felt a surge of pain in his chest. As he looked down, he saw the dark elf's spear lodged. It had been a direct hit to his heart and blood was pumping from the tiny hole.

Aerlyn, close on the heels of Zuboko, nimbly pulled a small vial from her leather pouch and dripped a milky liquid into the wound. Quickly and silently, the wound was healing. The puncture to the heart was closing and the life force that had been seeping away was now surging back into all the blood vessels and cells. In a short while, he would be fully healed and re-energised. If luck favoured them at all, the dark elf would not make another attack at Zuboko until the process had been completed.

Aerlyn heard the clang of steel behind her, her attention to Zuboko had left her exposed. Ice cold steel plunged into her back causing her to take a sharp intake of breath and to scream out in pain. Her attacker had not finished with her yet. The dark elf re-angled the spear that was still thrust into Aerlyn and sliced it at an angle severing her spinal column in one sharp and powerful movement. Immediately, she lost all feeling to her lower limbs and crimson blood cascaded from Aerlyn onto Zuboko and the already blood splattered ground.

Aerlyn was swiftly losing consciousness. Her eyes were clouded and her hearing was fuzzy. In the distance she could hear her name being called and she was aware that her heart was beating slower and slower but louder and louder as it tried to survive. Through her clouded vision she thought she could make out her brother Lexon. But Lexon was dead, surely? She could see the courtyard of stone where only a few hours ago life's daily activities had been taking place but now held only death and destruction. The bodies of priests and saints were strewn on the ground, many of them still clutching books of study in their now cold, lifeless hands.

For some reason, her eyes noticed a memorial statue that was inscribed with the words, 'This is a land of God; it shall never be forsaken'.

It just had been. The flags of the towers were torn and burnt. The ancient wall and the previously exquisite statues of the God Nemea lay smashed and shattered. The scrolls of enchantments that had been passed from generation to generation through the ages were now muddied and stained with the blood of their protectors. The church was still smouldering from the fires that had burnt within and the limp body of a priest was swinging eerily from the beams at its entrance.

Zuboko, although slowly recovering, was hardly breathing as he lay in the mud. Harthor was desperately trying to crawl up the muddy embankment towards the runic archway to gain height to make another attack on the formidable dark elf. He watched anxiously as Aerlyn, so close to death, was still being brutally attacked by the evil, dark elf. He could also hear the dark elf ranting at Aerlyn as he made the attacks. "Ha! Not so tough without your brother or father!" he crowed cockily giving Aerlyn another sharp kick.

Lexon was not dead. He was watching the devastating action from the keep where he had regained consciousness just in time to see the horrendous attack on his sister. Rage was growing inside him. Never had his family been so devastated or insulted by what he was witnessing now as the dark elf assaulted his dying sister. He scrabbled through the festering flesh of the piled corpses and dragged out a longbow. He ripped two spent arrows from the body of a dead orc and swiftly and expertly teased the feathers to ensure an accurate flight. He loaded the weapon and unleashed his attack. The shot was slightly off target and struck his sister's enemy in the hand, making the assailant recoil. Lexon cursed at the misjudged flight and reloaded the long bow. Just as he took aim, the dark elf was struck with a long bolt fired from a crossbow that Harthor had found as he climbed the runic archway and was now wielding and targeting again.

Harthor and Lexon fired simultaneously, both their weapons making perfect shots. The dark elf staggered, clutching at his chest, eyes rolling and fell against a crumbling wall. The added weight of the dark elf was too much for the weakened wall and what remained of it toppled covering the dark elf in a cloud of dust and rock.

Lexon was already dashing down the muddy embankment, slipping and sliding as he tried to support his smashed arm on the decent. As he reached Aerlyn, he pulled a red and gold amulet from inside his tunic. Lexon snapped the chain that supported the amulet and guided its glowing form over the gaping wound on Aerlyn's frail body. The wound opened up to disclose the extent of her injuries. When Lexon saw the shattered spine and lacerated organs, he winced with concern for his sister. She was barely breathing and her lips were tinged with the blue of death. The amulet shimmered and transfigured into a long rim; the rim floated into the oozing wound and repaired the damaged spine and organs. Lexon could see Aerlyn healing from deep within. Her breathing was becoming stronger and her heart began to beat with a regular, strong rhythm. Aerlyn slowly opened her eyes and Lexon held her close.

Harthor found the vial of healing fluid in the mud beside Zuboko and dripped a portion of the milky potion onto his wounded arm. It was healing well. Zuboko looked on, relieved to know that Aerlyn was saved.

Harthor made his way to the smouldering carcass of the church and cut down the swinging body of the priest. He laid him respectfully on the ground and offered his prayers for the deaths of the elves and humans that had perished in the attack.

Over the next day, the city became a graveyard as the city dwellers were buried and the enemy bodies were dragged outside the perimeter of the city grounds and burnt in large stinking mounds.

Aerlyn and Lexon buried their brothers and sisters with their ancestors in the family tomb. Their father, a true leader, was given as formal a passing as possible and entombed with the great elven leaders.

Having shown their respects to those that had lost their lives, the heroes returned to the pile of rubble where the dark elf had finally fallen. There was nothing, the body had gone.

The dark elf had limped quietly away, cursing his failure and already plotting his next attack.

The next day dawned bright and clear only making the devastation seem all the more bleak. Zuboko had retrieved the parts of his shattered sword and had given the task of reassembling the pieces to an ironmonger who they had found hiding for fear of his life in the dark, dank cellars. The ironmonger was hard at work. Sweat dripped from his brow as he crashed his heavy anvil onto the super heated metal of the sword. He lifted the reforged weapon into the air and closed one eye to gauge the splendour and accuracy of his work. Rubies glinted in the morning sunlight. Thrusting down the blade it sliced through a boulder like a knife through butter. The ironmonger smiled to himself. It was a remarkable sword and he called to Zuboko to confirm his success.

Lexon was busily loading supplies of weapons and food into a large sack. He packed all he could salvage; daggers, arrows, potions, the whole works. Hurling the sack and its heavy contents over his broad shoulder, Lexon made his way swiftly towards the Temple of Kairon, the worship place for the God of Invincibility. He kept his head low and hoped that the citadel dwellers that had survived the battle and, more importantly, the heroes did not notice his departure. Lexon had slept poorly following the battle, suffering terrible dreams of Aerlyn and her bloody body, dead. His subconscious had reminded him of the creatures still hidden in the destroyed citadel siege towers. He would finish the job that had been so destructively started the day before.

"Where are you going?" Aerlyn asked.

Lexon, disappointed at being noticed turned to see all the heroes watching his exit towards the runic archway. "I'm leaving! I work solo!" he retorted aggressively.

"No you are not! If you don't stay with us, then I am coming with you!" Aerlyn stormed, equally aggressive with her hands firmly on her hips.

"Me too!" chipped in Zuboko.

"And don't forget me!" called Harthor.

Lexon stood very still looking at each of the heroes in turn and finally at the stubborn face of his sister. A grim smile slowly turned the corners of his mouth. The heroes embraced. A new alliance had been formed.

. Chapter Nine .

AN OLD ACQUAINTANCE

DEEP in a temple, a skirmish began. Harthor had already made contact with the enemy and had his sword deeply embedded in the tentacled orc's membrane. A puddle of green acid blood burned into the stone, sending up a cloud of pungent green smoke. The orc's defence was incredibly toxic and in an effort not to come into contact with the deadly blood, Harthor was bludgeoning the creature with his shield. Every blow was with Harthor's full force and the beast soon succumbed.

Lexon, battling two mutants simultaneously, ducked and dived swiftly avoiding each of the attacks. With one agile movement, he crashed their two skulls together. Immediately, their limp bodies fell to the floor and dissolved in a puddle of acid blood. Lexon, in a nimble bound, avoided the deadly slime and leapt onto the base of a statue.

Zuboko raised his staff into the air. A mighty howl of wind blew the dust from the floor. It swirled faster and faster. The enemy were blinded and covered their eyes in pain. Blundering and unaware of their exposure, the beasts met their final doom as Aerlyn unleashed a hail of arrows.

Harthor turned and surveyed the damage. No creature moved. Harthor knelt and prayed to Epelorn. As he leaned his huge torso forward, apparently deep in concentration, an unnoticed demon reared forwards and prepared to sink its foul, razor teeth into the cleric's face. In mid-strike the demon froze and whimpered in pain. Looking down at its stomach, it saw the mighty shaft of Harthor's weapon. Even when deep in prayer, Harthor was prepared for ambush and had cast a protection spell prior to his worship of the great Gods. Harthor's sword had responded to the threat and had levitated and plunged into the dark depths of the creature's gut. The beast inhaled one last breath and keeled over onto the degenerating carcass of one of its allies. Harthor continued to pray, apparently oblivious to the attack.

"Comoq demons! Always a pain in the rear" Lexon grinned smugly, wiping gunge from his leather tunic.

"It'll never come out!" Aerlyn chortled. Whilst Harthor continued his prayers of thankfulness, the other heroes checked the bodies of their enemies. They were surprised to find vast amounts of gold and gems. The heroes knew that Comoq demons were notorious for looting but this amount of treasure had to be some kind of bounty for services rendered. There could be only one person behind this further attack. Ladracsin!

Harthor's meditation came to a sudden end. Head still bowed, he lumbered to his broad feet and to everyone's surprise, he disappeared through the gateway calling that he would return soon and that he felt there was still unfinished business.

Zuboko made to follow his companion but Harthor raised a calloused hand and said, "I will sort this myself, stay!" Zuboko shrugged and continued to examine the fallen beasts. He rolled over the body of a particularly smelly Comoq and saw embedded in the flesh of its blistered chest a glittering rune. The rune of the Comoq God, Pakita Keabera. The rune, which had been circular in shape, was now split in two as Harthor had penetrated its smooth surface during the attack. This Comoq was a cultist druid. Ladracsin meant business.

The heroes remained in the temple waiting for the return of Harthor. They didn't have to wait long. Harthor burst through the doorway; scarred, bloody and clasped in his hand was the decapitated head of a stricken Comoq demon. Smiling, Harthor held the head up and joked foolishly, "If we survive this, I'm having this hung up in my chambers in Richareme!" He watched some ooze drizzle down his blade and drip onto the floor and continued, "There were a few more demons trying to escape and I found a gang of goblins and orcs. I killed many and took my trinket!" he said as he jiggled the head back and forth. Slime dripped from where it had been severed and, with the movement, flew and landed on Lexon's leather tunic. Aerlyn laughed as Lexon rolled his eyes at yet more gloop on his clothes. "Sorry!" exclaimed Harthor, casting the head aside.

The group collected their belongings and trekked through the maze of dungeons and sewers that ran beneath the temple. The smell was rancid and caused them to cough and retch. Their route was dark and dank. The scuttling of rats echoed through the chambers. The usually graceful Aerlyn tripped while leading the way. The body of a wounded and dying refugee was hunched at the side of the tunnel, supported by an archway, his eyes pointed unnaturally upwards to the ceiling where the heroes saw the eerie shape of a Soul Eater floating.

Entranced, the heroes watched, unable to resist, as the spiritual, luminescent ghost circled above the poor peasant. The air was icy and a chill rippled down their spines. Rooted to the spot and unable to help the doomed peasant, the heroes watched as the peasant's mouth gaped open, displaying rotten, black teeth. A wisp of white smoke floated from his mouth, twisting onwards and upwards towards the Soul Eater. The Soul Eater sucked at the white smoke and the two were joined, mouth to mouth.

As the white smoke spiralled into the Soul Eater, its iridescence grew whilst the peasant aged in seconds. His skin wrinkled and dried, all previous muscular tone disappeared and his skin shrivelled and disintegrated to reveal a dry white skeleton. As the Soul Eater sucked the last remaining remnants of soul and spirit from the poor man, his bones turned to dust.

As the bones dusted, the Soul Eater's hypnotic spell over the heroes dissipated and Aerlyn, quickest to respond, drew her bow and swiftly strung a silver artistic arrow. She aimed high but the spirit was no longer there. Behind her came a gargling moan; as she turned, she realised that the Soul Eater had taken on the corporeal form of the peasant, only without a soul and it was slowly, jerkily, making its way towards the heroes. Aerlyn, suddenly frozen at the ghoulish appearance of the possessed peasant, failed to release her arrow. Instead, the mighty blade of Harthor jabbed at the staggering zombie's ribcage. It stalled its progress momentarily before the zombie continued to make its way forwards. A boiling, red flame screeched from Zuboko's staff and scorched the flesh on the creature's chest. The chamber was filled with a disgusting aroma of burning skin and the sizzle of melting fat. The beast recoiled back but only for a few seconds and then continued on its relentless path towards the heroes. Lexon threw a vial at the zombie. It fractured on impact and a stream of pure acid covered its legs. The creature moaned and the acid rapidly burned through the flesh and bone of its legs until only a torso remained on the ground. The creature started to drag what remained of its body ever forward at the heroes, scratching and clawing its nails along the rocks. This creature was unstoppable. Harthor kicked out with all his might, knocking the zombie onto its back and then thrust his holy cross onto the demons heart. The cross burned deep but the zombie kept on coming. Aerlyn, now recomposed, sent a hail of arrows, each making a hit. The creature's body spasmed with each hit and groaned like a weary predator but dragged itself onwards.

The heroes now had their backs at the wall and all of their efforts appeared futile. Just as Harthor raised his sword, to slice the zombie into as many pieces as possible, huge green vines burst through the ground and entwined the remaining limbs of the zombie. The vines coiled tighter and tighter. More erupted from the ground and circled the creature's neck and torso. Every part of the zombie was encased in tightening vines. The pressure increased and the zombie exploded.

Singed flesh and green slimy vine peppered the walls of the chamber and the heroes. Zuboko had thought of an ingenious method of zombie disposal. The other heroes turned to Zuboko and then looked down at their heavily stained clothes. Laughter echoed through the chamber!

The laughter subsided and Lexon picked up a small pack that had belonged to the peasant. Looking inside, he commented," Not many worldly goods; a few coins, a patch of ragged fabric and a dagger!"

"Another being on the long list of people that have suffered from this festering evil. Another to avenge" growled Harthor.

The exhausted band made their way further along the warren of tunnels striding through gunge and slipping on slime.

Lexon, who was leading the group, suddenly stopped and held up his hand to cause the others to stop. They all stood quietly, even holding their breath so as not to make a sound. Lexon's keen elven hearing had not let him down and he continued to listen to sounds coming from the darkness ahead. It was a voice cursing.

"Come on you swine-bags! Wretched vermin! We've got to get to the surface before those do-gooders find us!" The sound of a blade, crashed angrily onto a shield, echoed around.

Lexon peered around the wall just as a foul orc leader stood in readiness to leave. Their eyes made contact and without hesitation the orc bellowed out the alarm, "Scumballs! It's one of them scumballs!"

The heroes withdrew behind the shelter of the wall, weapons raised and ready to retaliate. Lexon had counted about nine goblins in a tight group but he was unsure as to how many orcs there could be. Ear piercing screams and screeches pulsated around the tunnels as the enemy prepared to attack. Then they were there. Zuboko smashed his sword into the nearest orc as it ran towards him. The orc parried the attack but its weapon was made only of wood and splintered on impact, now useful only for firewood. The orc's face visibly crumpled as he realised his fate; Zuboko plunged his sword deep inside the orc. Aerlyn, though exhausted, was on fine form and sent arrow after arrow to find its target.

The enemy fell quickly and in the confined space of the tunnel, the mounting bodies were making moving and fighting very difficult. Five remaining goblins stood tight together, shields held high forming a protective wall. Aerlyn's arrows and Zuboko's magic volleyed against the shield wall but made little if any impact and merely rebounded. One of the goblins broke ranks and charged at the heroes, a menacing axe held high ready to chop, and roaring louder and louder with every step as he drew closer to his targets. A silver tipped bolt scorched through the stagnant air and ripped through his weak leather armour embedding itself right in the creature's heart. The creature fell to the floor, flinching and twitching. The goblin's actions had left his colleagues exposed. Two of them turned and fled along the narrow tunnel. The others were not so quick in their thoughts or actions and Zuboko unleashed a raging firebolt from his staff which incinerated the goblins within a white hot flame in seconds.

Harthor made chase along the tunnels, tracking the two goblins that had escaped. As he splashed through the murky water, his foot caught on something solid. Harthor stopped abruptly and, to his surprise, saw the bodies of the two escaped goblins. From their chests he saw the long shaft of an arrow from a longbow. Even in the tunnel's gloom he could see the glinting jewel encrusted feathers. A memory, deep in Harthor's mind, struggled to the surface. He had seen these unusual and extravagant arrows before. Cryslow!

Cryslow had once been a human. He had been tempted by treasures and jewels and had readily sold his soul to a Demon God in exchange for unlimited wealth. What Cryslow hadn't bargained for was having his skin transformed into a gem shell with the amazing hardness of the ultimate gem stone, diamond.

The mark of the Demon God, the shape of a hammer, had formed on his forehead, and even though Cryslow was as rich as he had ever wished, he was in fact a slave. A slave to the Demon God who had bought his soul.

Harthor had encountered Cryslow a long time ago when he and Zuboko had just joined forces. Their meeting had taken place in the Silvermine gorge in the south of Galgir. The evil Demi-God, Demite, had been steadily building an army and had plans to conquer Richareme. Cryslow, who was deeply and madly in love with the beautiful and powerful Demi-God, was at the Silvermine gorge helping his evil beloved to create a devastating army. Harthor and Zuboko had caught them off guard and poorly prepared and taken an easy victory. During the bloody battle, Demite had been slain and had died in much pain in the devastated Cryslow's arms. Cryslow had vowed to avenge her death mercilessly.

As the memories flooded back, Harthor then saw ahead of him the glimmering jewel skin of Cryslow and his deadly, jewel covered beech long bow.

"So this is what you have become! The great Harthor chasing runaways in dank tunnels!" growled Cryslow in a gravelly rough voice.

Cryslow had not changed at all. Piercing, ice like eyes stared at Harthor. For a second, Cryslow's attention was distracted as the rest of the heroes came running up to Harthor's side.

"Ah I see that the two of you still keep each other's company, Zuboko! Taking my revenge on the two of you will be very satisfying" continued Cryslow.

Aerlyn and Lexon had never encountered the likes of Cryslow before and drew their weapons in readiness. Cryslow looked scathingly at the weapons and laughed out loud.

"Who's this jerk?" asked Lexon. With surprising speed, Cryslow was at Lexon's side and had his tough, shimmering hand firmly around his throat. With very little effort, he lifted

Lexon by the neck until his legs twitched and thrashed to support himself on something. His face changed to a dark puce colour and he struggled to draw breath.

"I don't like you already, dragon slop!" Cryslow growled menacingly at Lexon. Immediately Aerlyn leapt to her brother's defence. She snatched at her dagger and then froze in a trance.

Years ago, on the fateful day that she passed to the other side, Demite had bequeathed a special power to Cryslow; the power to control the minds of females. As a consequence, since her passing, Cryslow had had no issue with female attention either willing or non-willing as slaves. It now appeared that Cryslow had not lost his touch over time and at this very moment he was controlling the will of Aerlyn.

Aerlyn suddenly pulled Lexon away from Cryslow's mighty grip and hurled him bodily at the wall behind them. Lexon smashed into the rock and plummeted to the ground much the worse for wear and dazed at the sudden attack from his sister. Aerlyn smiled down at the broken body of her brother, but her eyes were cold. There was no remorse or compassion in her smile. Aerlyn then turned and wrapped her limber arms around the solid gem stone body of Cryslow and passionately caressed his strong arm. Both Zuboko and Harthor were motionless and speechless at this outrageous behaviour from their comrade. Harthor's jaw dropped and Zuboko simply stared. Through utter surprise, neither attempted to assist Lexon who was now struggling to sit himself uncomfortably against the wall that had caused him so much pain. The pain was too much and the weakened Lexon fell into unconsciousness. Aerlyn turned and snarled at her companions. Cryslow smirked at his enemy and then drew his attention to Aerlyn, watching her with cold, deceiving eyes.

Cryslow bent his massive torso and whispered into Aerlyn's delicate ear, "Darling, it is time to get mad!"

Harthor knew exactly what was going to happen next. Aerlyn gazed up worshipfully at Cryslow and slowly stroked her hand along his broad, streamlined chest. Changing her gaze to Harthor, she casually made her way across the tunnel toward Harthor and gently kissed him on the cheek. "Sorry honey" she purred, "I'm going to have to kill you!" In a reflex action Aerlyn's limber leg flashed forwards and her foot kicked Harthor in the centre of his face. Blood spurted from his nose and large tears dropped from his eyes. Slightly dazed by the swiftness of the action and the surprising strength of the blow, Harthor stood, clasping his face as blood continued to flow freely. Zuboko's complete attention had been taken by Aerlyn's attack on Harthor and he had not noticed Cryslow swiftly and soundlessly moving in for an attack. Cryslow's curled fist exploded onto Zuboko's jaw and sent him reeling across the tunnel. Zuboko dropped to the floor, motionless. A second strike from Cryslow sent the dazed Harthor to his knees and Aerlyn followed through with a knee to his swollen face. Harthor fell forwards onto the sodden ground.

All three warriors, oblivious to their surroundings, now lay unconscious; a restless slumber, haunted by vivid images of the turned Aerlyn and an uncomfortable sensation that they were lying in something wet.

. Chapter Ten .

AERLYN TO THE RESCUE

LEXON was the first of the heroes to rouse from the slumber. Every part of his body ached with even the slightest movement. He tentatively lifted his blood smeared head and looked around at his surroundings as they slowly came into focus. His fingers automatically reached down for his weapons but he could not feel any. He had no form of defence; his only consolation was that he had not been restrained in any way, even though he could see chains and handcuffs hanging from the dark, dank wall of the room. Lexon tried to move his position and flinched as a searing pain shot through his leg. As his eyes became used to the dismal amount of light in the room, he could see a shard of glass jabbing from his thigh. He crawled his fingers towards the glass to pull it from his flesh when he noticed the strange shape that had been etched into his skin. The skin on his chest was raw and seeped in blood, but even in the weak light he could just about make out the shape of a hammer crusted in dried blood.

Lying next to Lexon, Harthor started to wake. He groaned as he started to move his massive bulk. He, too, had had all of his weapons removed, had been stripped of his shirt and branded with the sign of a hammer to his chest. Zuboko was still unconscious and Harthor reached out a battered hand to shake and try to rouse the defenceless wizard. Just as Zuboko was starting to show signs of life, light footsteps could be heard from the corridor. All three heroes drew a sharp intake of breath and stayed still trying to appear that they were still unconscious. The heavy wooden door creaked as it opened and a stream of light silhouetted a figure in the doorway.

Lexon, unable to resist, opened an eye to assess his imprisoner. To his shock, it was Aerlyn. It was Aerlyn, but not the kind, gentle sister he recognised. This Aerlyn was dressed from head to toe in tight leather and her hair had been styled into a range of spikes. She too was branded with the hammer mark but hers was to the forehead, just as Cryslow himself had been marked. Lexon released his breath in dismay. His sister had been overcome by the evil of Cryslow. But, just as he lifted his head to take a better look, Aerlyn changed; she was back to the old Aerlyn that he loved and trusted. Could it be true? Was Aerlyn good or evil? The questions buzzed around Lexon's brain. In answer to those questions, Aerlyn smiled sweetly at her brother.

"Aerlyn!" whispered Lexon. At Lexon's exclamation the other two heroes peered at the person before them.

"Yes!" breathed Aerlyn gently. "Listen, we don't have much time. I've been trying to find Cryslow's weaknesses. It's been tough. The mind control thing held only for a short time; it only has a lasting effect on humans. So, erm, so I've had to pretend. I managed to salvage a cloaking charm, however, from Zuboko's bag. It seems to be working"

"So wait a minute, you actually were yourself when you put that stuff on?" Lexon smirked.

"Yes! It'll be a nightmare to get my hair back to normal and, oh I never realised how uncomfortable such tight leather could be!" Aerlyn chuckled back, glad to see her brother and her comrades. "He's got at least ten other slaves and they are really pretty!"

Together in the dank, dark prison, they worked together to forge a plan to defeat Cryslow. Aerlyn had been very cunning in undertaking the company of Cryslow. The initial mind control had soon worn off and Cryslow had excused her from his presence. His slaves had transferred the three heroes to the locked room and Aerlyn had been careful to hide their weapons and clothes from the sight of the other slaves. She hadn't been able to stop the branding process and had felt most distressed at the thought of her friends and the pain they were suffering. She needn't have worried, as they had remained unconscious throughout the whole procedure.

Still, she felt pangs of guilt as she saw the gross scars they had left. These would be marks that would endure a lifetime.

Harthor tentatively pulled on his shirt and armour over the hammer branding, wincing as he tightened the straps of leather. Lexon, feeling much better having had a good slug of Zuboko's healing potion, was loading himself with all the weapons he could carry. He would be in the guise of a female slave, protected, just like Aerlyn, by a cloaking spell. Zuboko prepared himself to launch a sneak attack. They were ready. Aerlyn gave them a quick, but detailed plan of the fortified building that Cryslow had built as a temple to his beloved departed Demi-God Demite; the temple that now served as his headquarters.

The heroes set out; first, they had to crawl through a man sized storm drain. It was no problem for Aerlyn and Lexon; their thin bodies moving smoothly. Even Zuboko was managing without too much trouble, but the sheer size of Harthor gave him very little space to move his bulk, let alone crawl; it was hard work and beads of sweat ran down Harthor's brow as he inched along the tight tunnel.

The tunnel became slightly lighter as daylight showed through the grilled cover of the drain inlet. A ladder of metal steps lead up towards the light and Lexon climbed them swiftly. Lifting the edge of the cover, he carefully tried to see signs of the enemy. His alert eyes noticed the slight frame of a woman, ornately dressed in gold chiffon and draped with jewels. She had to be one of Cryslow's slaves. Slowly he lowered the cover until she had passed. Then, sliding the cover back soundlessly, Lexon mustered all his strength and jumped clear of the tunnel and moved agilely to the shadows of the nearest wall. The others quickly followed. Harthor, relieved to be at the end of the tunnel, breathed deeply to refresh the oxygen in his previously constricted lungs. His huge hand wiped the sweat from his forehead. The group slowly inched their way along the wall and all froze when they heard a man's voice greeting the arrival of another woman. They heard a door close and continued to edge their way along. Harthor stepped forwards and took the guard by surprise. With one sharp twist and a crack, the guard fell to the floor, his neck turned in an unnatural position. There appeared to be no further guards and Aerlyn took the lead walking through the unguarded hall. A slave girl, spotting Aerlyn in a state of disarray, having scrambled through the dirty tunnel, came towards her.

"Where do you think you're going?" she questioned Aerlyn aggressively. Aerlyn had grown to know these women in the short time since their arrival and pitied them, for they had no control over their actions. The woman, smelling sweetly of perfume, came closer to Aerlyn. With regret, Aerlyn grabbed her and thrust the woman's body over her bent knee. The woman's frail frame slumped to the ground.

The heroes were in the slave womens' chamber, which was the antechamber to Cryslow's quarters. At the disturbance, the other women turned to see Aerlyn and the dead woman. As one, they swooped, weapons drawn. Aerlyn recalled that one of the main mind control imperatives was to protect Cryslow at all costs, even with their lives. The other heroes rushed forwards to assist Aerlyn as the slaves swarmed down on her.

At the commotion, a vast door at the far side of the antechamber swung open, its hinges creaking with the weight of the wood. As the doors crashed onto the stone walls, the huge figure of Cryslow stepped forwards. If he was surprised to find the ambush, he did not show it. He simply marched forwards into the thick of it. Fearlessly, Aerlyn unleashed a flurry of arrows as he made his way towards her. He brushed them away like twigs. Cryslow curled his mighty fingers into a fist and plunged them at the base of a statue which smashed into rubble. He picked up the body of the statue as a weapon and hurled it at Zuboko.

Zuboko parried the strike but the sheer weight of rock crushed his arm and sent Zuboko catapulting across the room. Harthor goaded Cryslow, who readily took the challenge. Cryslow lunged at Harthor. In his eagerness, he missed his footing and roared as he plummeted to the ground.

With all of his brute strength, Harthor leaned against a towering statue. The plan was working. Aerlyn rushed to help Harthor and she too heaved with all her might, her tiny feet resting on the statue's base and her back pressed firmly against a neighbouring figure. Taking a deep breath, she pushed with all the strength she could muster. There was an audible grinding sound and the statue started to move. They had to be quick. Cryslow had also realised what the heroes were trying to do but his movements were cumbersome and he was struggling to get to his feet. With another surge of strength, the statue they were pushing started to slide forwards. It teetered as the bulk of its weight moved beyond the pedestal and with an eerie silence, it leaned and tumbled to the ground. Cryslow raised a protective arm but it was too late. The crumbling rock fell directly onto Cryslow. The rock smashed against the gemstone shell of Cryslow's skin, causing huge cracks to ripple across his body. Instantly, his very core exploded, sending a shower of diamond cut stones across the room in every direction. Cryslow had been destroyed; destroyed by the very thing that he most loved. Demite! The statue had been of Demite and it had been told in legend that the only thing that could ever destroy Cryslow would be his beloved. Most had therefore considered Cryslow to be indestructible as Demite had been long dead. None could have imagined that the statue of Demite would have proven to be Cryslow's doom.

. Chapter Eleven .

THE RISING

THE heroes had salvaged what they could in the way of provisions and weapons from Cryslow's castle; they were now rested and had resumed their quest to destroy the evil of Ladracsin.

They had been travelling for a day and a night. Lexon stared out across the vast forest that lay ahead of them. It was not going to be a fun trip.

To add to his dismay, dark clouds had been gathering overhead, there was thunder in the air and electricity crackled through the sky. With an almighty clap of thunder, the heavens opened and rain hailed down. It poured through the tree canopy, which gave them no protection, and soon streams of water were gushing down the hillside. The earth became swamp like and made walking treacherous. Even the nimble Aerlyn and Lexon were struggling. Suddenly the group turned, startled at Harthor's cry, as he slipped down the hillside in a torrent of water and mud. Soon he was out of sight, unable to grasp at plant life to stop his speedy descent down to the valley below. The others looked at each other and ruefully shrugged as they launched themselves after Harthor down the hillside via the mud slides.

They all descended rapidly and landed in a muddy mass at the foot of the slope. Coughing and spluttering, they emerged from the mud. Covered head to toe in brown slime, they dragged their heavy bodies to a drier section of undergrowth. Laughing, Harthor grinned at his companions, "That was fun!"

The other three turned to Harthor, faces dead pan, with mud dripping from each of them. After a second, all their mouths broke into smiles and they roared with laughter at the state of each other. When the laughter had subsided, the group looked around their resting place to get their bearings and to see if there was anywhere to wash themselves. Close by, they could see a few hut dwellings. Maybe a tiny village. They would go and ask for washing facilities and food. Their bags had been soaked through and their rations contaminated with mud and water. It did not take the heroes long to reach the village but what met their eyes on their arrival was not what they had expected.

They moved quietly around the perimeter of the tiny village. They did not want to scare the occupants whilst in their muddy state, but they were also cautious not to be made captive by any enemy that may have seized the village.

What met their eyes saddened them deeply. The whole village had been slaughtered and bodies lay scattered everywhere. More of Ladracsin's evil. When would this stop?

Having checked the buildings for any of the murderers, the heroes set about burying the corpses. It was a sorrowful task; the whole village had been shown no mercy. The rain continued to beat down as they dug in the mud and marked the areas with mounds of rocks and crosses made from lashing wood with rope. As each grave was sealed, Harthor mumbled words of passage for the deceased.

As Harthor stood at the foot of one burial mound, head bent in respect and prayer, the rocks began to move. Was it his imagination? He looked closer. Yes, they were moving. Harthor was just about to call to Aerlyn when a hand thrust through the rocks. It clawed and reached up skyward. As Harthor watched, he realised that the person in the grave must not have been dead. Without hesitation he rushed to the moving pile of rocks and started to dig to release the buried person. The rest of the heroes splashed over to see what was happening and they too tried to release the person.

With relief, they saw the top of the person's head and cleared the earth from its face. The scrabbling hands grabbed at Harthor and dragged him close so that they were face to face. Harthor looked into the person's eyes. They were lifeless. This was not a person buried alive. This was a zombie. Harthor reeled away, just in time as the zombie tried to take a chunk of flesh from Harthor's cheek.

"Oh, my God!" Aerlyn shrieked, her face ashen. "Quick, collect your things we must leave."

Harthor raised his sword, "God save us all!" he roared as he brought the sharp blade down across the neck of the writhing zombie and sliced off its head. The body became motionless. Harthor's relief was short lived. At every burial plot, the rocks were starting to move. The heroes gazed around them. Scratching, scrabbling hands thrust through the soaked earth.

From the forest behind the heroes, came a moaning, groaning sound. They turned to face an army of zombies staggering and lurching their lifeless limbs towards them. Each zombie bore the wounds of its unfortunate death, dragging severed legs and arms with them. The heroes were frozen with the horror of what advanced towards them.

Zuboko, the first to react, raised his staff and cast a light spell at the ever advancing zombies. The fiends slowed for only seconds as the intense, bright light spell melted their flesh. It did not stop them.

The heroes drew their weapons and cut and hacked at the creatures. Creatures that, but a few minutes ago, they had greatly pitied and for whom they had felt compassion at their destruction. What was this evil that turned the victims into flesh eating machines?

Aerlyn's arrows were useless and the zombies kept coming. The only thing that stopped them was to cut their heads off. Hastily Aerlyn abandoned her bow and grabbed at her dagger as a zombie in the form of an old man bore down on her. Aerlyn plunged the dagger into the zombie's skull, penetrating deep into its brain and central nervous system. All motion ceased and the zombie rolled lifeless to the mud.

The heroes, though destroying many of the zombies, were heavily outnumbered. Harthor had lost a lot of blood and staggered wearily against a nearby wall collapsing at the mercy of the advancing zombies. The nightmarish demons lunged at Harthor's unprotected neck. As they bent to feed on the scrambling Harthor, one by one, the evil creatures turned to dust. Harthor looked down at his exposed chest and there, glinting, was his holy cross. Passed down from his father's ancestors through the ages. The holy cross had saved another in Harthor's line. It had saved Harthor's life.

Aerlyn, Zuboko and Lexon seized their chance and dashed to help Harthor. They hauled his great bulk upright, slipping and sliding in the mud and made their way to the protection of a desecrated church building. The hanging torso of a priest jittered and jerked in a vain attempt to attack them, as they passed. Slamming the huge wooden door behind them and strengthening it with a wooden beam, Zuboko helped Harthor with the scrolls of Epelorn. Aerlyn and Lexon swiftly made their way around the inside of the tiny church, checking that the building was secure against the marauding zombies that had now made their way to the perimeter wall of the church.

Unrolling the vast pieces of parchment, yellowed with age and torn with use, Harthor mustered the last of his energy and bellowed an incantation to restore the church to holy land. They would be safe from the evils that roamed outside. At least for a while.

As the incantation took effect, the unholy corpse of the hanging priest withered and shrivelled away; he had been suspended over the holy grounds of the church.

Lexon, returning from checking the security of the church, made his way to where Harthor and Zuboko had stopped to read the incantation. His keen eyes were drawn to strange mystical markings inked in red on the reverse of the incantation parchment. It was a warlock's incantation.

Terror spread over Lexon's face as he realised that the warlock's incantation had been initiated simultaneously as Harthor had bellowed the Epelorn incantation.

"Run!" Lexon roared at his fellow heroes as he hastily launched himself bodily at the doorway. Harthor summoned all his reserves of strength and all three heroes followed Lexon, launching themselves in the same direction.

Still in mid-air, the heroes felt the church explode behind them and a rush of blue flames scorch past them consuming the oxygen in a massive fire ball. Dazed and sprawled once again in the mud, the heroes turned as they heard a spine chilling peel of laughter ring across the landscape from the direction of the west tower. Scrambling, they looked up to see a warlock dressed in white and gold. His long mane of hair was also white and from his chin, hung a long beard.

"Ha, ha, ha! I am Numbar!! The new God! The new true Lord!" He roared down as he surveyed the crowd of undead.

Aerlyn reached for an arrow. Just as she reached the lethal weapon, she suddenly began to feel very strange. The hordes of undead that were now still and gazing up towards the tower to where the warlock stood, arms outstretched, seemed to come in and out of focus. Sound had become distorted. Aerlyn felt sick to her stomach and unable to move. Her head became heavy and her eyes started to close. Just as her head came to rest on the ground, she turned to see that Harthor, Zuboko and Lexon were also motionless and already had their eyes closed. Unable to fight the sleepiness any longer, Aerlyn passed into a deep sleep.

. Chapter Twelve .

THE CITY OF KRAKARA

LEXON awoke. His joints ached as he was jolted and jostled. The surface on which he lay was firm but moving and had a strong, damp odour. Lying very still, Lexon slowly opened his eyes. The glare was intense and he struggled to resist from calling out in pain. Again, even more slowly, he squinted into the bright sunlight. His senses were reeling. All around him were voices and chants, crashes and bangs. Where was he? Suddenly his last memories sprang into his head. Well, he hadn't been consumed by zombies anyway, so that was a bonus.

Continuing to lie very still, Lexon tried to see where he was and what was going on around him. He had never been to this place before but recalled being told of the city of multiraces; he must be in the ancient city of Krakara.

He saw by a wall a gang of ratmen mugging a half elf. The ratmen were vicious creatures. Pointed faces with prominent teeth snapped at the victim while razor sharp claws scratched and maimed. Thick, hairless tails swished like snakes about to strike. The half elf did not stand a chance and was soon lying, bloody and in pain while the attackers made off with their spoils. Passers-by seemed unperturbed by the scuffle.

The streets were busy, with strange looking creatures moving in all directions. The roads were covered in filth and stank of death and decay. Another scuffle between a troll and a Volksorc spilled from the path into the road, close to where the cart carrying Lexon slowly trundled along. The Volksorc, a creature with the body of an orc and head of a vulture, stood strong against the troll. Almost as soon as the tussle started, it was smothered by the presence of several armour clad zombies who piled onto the troll and dragged him away.

Lexon still felt he should not move so as not to draw attention to his consciousness. He was not sure whether his fellow heroes were with him or indeed if it was only he that had survived. Just as he resolved to move, the cart came to a halt. Lexon heard the driver making the cart fast and dismounting. Lexon was aware that a crowd was starting to gather around the cart. He could make out dark elves in brown scaled rags with large hoods drooping over their heads and casting a shadow over their faces.

A piercing cry rang over the crowd that had gathered around the cart. The crowd were watching Lexon and eager to hear what the cart driver had to say.

Lexon carefully turned his gaze to where the majority of the crowd were looking. Stood on the edge of the cart was a strange being. Completely white and covered with iridescent scales was an elf sized lizard. Even his eyes were white and, as he surveyed the increasing crowd, a forked tongue whipped in and out of his lipless mouth.

The piercing cry rang out again. "Sssslaves for ssssale! Only ten sssssilver coinsssss for each!"

Lexon was to be sold as a slave; to the highest bidder! Unable to remain still any longer, Lexon tried to jump up but was immediately snatched back down to the cart. He looked to his wrists and ankles; he was shackled like an animal. An animal at a market. The shackles were attached to heavy iron chains.

The crowd laughed as Lexon tried to stand again, and again he was forced back to the cart.

"A feissssssty one that one, lotssss of energy!" roared the lizard creature, his tongue excitedly flicking back and forth.

"Lie sssstill, you dog!" muttered the creature, poking Lexon sharply with his staff "Be grateful Minisssster Numbar had pressssing mattersss elssssswhere and had no time to check that you were put to death; I will make a tidy profit ssssselling you assss a sssslave!"

An old hag, dressed in stained rags and a cloak that flowed from her head to the floor, elbowed her way to the front of the crowd. She liked what she saw and was keen to make a purchase today. But only if the price was right.

"Ah, this one would make an excellent slave for my guild," she warbled to no-one in particular.

"Excccellent choiccce madam. Would you like him collared firssssst?" The lizardman was eager to create some interest in his merchandise and even keener to make a sale.

Lexon didn't like the idea of being sold and he liked the idea of being sold to an old hag much less. He was relieved when she declined to have him collared, but his heart missed a beat as the crone asked the all too obliging lizardman to have a mind control tattoo placed on his back prior to purchase.

"Excccellent choiccce my dear!" grovelled the lizardman.

The lizardman moved lightly over other limbs shackled to the cart and grasped Lexon by the shoulder, pinching the flesh with his talons. He thrust Lexon face down and Lexon breathed the acrid scent of the wooden cart. Seconds later, a searing pain burnt into the middle of his back. Lexon roared out in pain. His flesh sizzled as the tattoo was emblazoned. A lipless smile came to the lizardman's face as he took the money from the hag, who too was smiling; only her smile displayed an uneven row of black and shattered teeth.

As the money passed into the taloned hand of the lizardman, the shackles to Lexon's wrists and ankles disappeared as though they had never been there; he was hurled from the cart by an invisible force and landed in the squalor at the hag's feet. Still in pain and dazed from his descent from the cart, Lexon looked up and into the black, soulless eyes of his owner. What did the future hold for Lexon now? With sudden realisation that he had not seen or heard any of the other heroes whilst his sale was in progress, Lexon turned to where he had fallen from the cart, hoping to see Aerlyn, Zuboko or Harthor. To his surprise, there was nothing but a dispersing crowd; there was no cart and there was no slave selling lizardman.

The hag jerked at the rope around Lexon's neck, pulling him forwards and he was forced to follow, as the old hag made her way through the street. Rounding the corner into a narrow alleyway, Lexon was surprised as the stooping hag broke into a nimble run and Lexon was forced to quicken his pace. Without warning, the woman stopped, the rope went slack and Lexon was just about to hurtle into the hag, when she suddenly dropped to the ground; the whole of her body disappearing into a dark hole that lead deep into the sewer system of the old town.

The rope pulled tight again and Lexon careered headlong into the dank drain. Landing heavily in the darkness, Lexon was unable to see at first, but as his keen eyes became accustomed to the dim and dreary light, he could make out the figures of both men and creatures. A loud, grinding noise was close by and as Lexon turned he saw many men in low grade armour, sharpening blunt swords on whirring grindstone blocks. Sparks and flashes ignited the air as the stone rendered the swords razor sharp. Further along the tunnel, Lexon could see reams of spears that had been loaded into traps. Close by, an enormous half orc was crashing a massive mallet onto sheets of steel, forging shield after shield. The heat from its fire was intense and great balls of sweat rolled down the orc's bulging biceps and sizzled into steam.

Again, the rope pulled tight, cutting deep into Lexon's neck which was now red with blood. With a sudden jerk, Lexon was pulled down to his knees, bashing them on jagged stones as he fell. In front of him, stood the biggest black troll that Lexon had ever seen. The troll was so huge that he was forced to crouch in the constraints of the sewer tunnel.

"I see you have found us another recruit!" he growled at the hag, whilst looking Lexon up and down, his face showing the disdain and contempt that all trolls felt towards elves. Hatred glinted in his soulless eyes.

"He's a member of the Dagorland clan!" retorted the old hag, jerking at the rope again and enjoying Lexon's discomfort.

"I see!" the troll growled and turned and walked away. The ground vibrated at every step he made.

Dragging Lexon roughly deeper into the darkness, with her mouth twisting as she spoke, revealing her blackened teeth, she sarcastically welcomed Lexon to his new home.

"Welcome to the rebel alliance against Minister Numbar. We believe that this empire should be a community!" Snapping the rope tight yet again, the hag cackled as she watched Lexon sprawl to the floor once more.

Lexon's head cracked on the slime covered wall and he moaned in pain. He scrambled to the wall and leaned against it, clasping his hand to the lump that was now erupting on his forehead. As he sighed at his plight, a cool hand grasped his. The hand was small and surprisingly soft. He turned to acknowledge the owner and looked straight into the eyes of his sister. Stunned, their mouths slowly broke into smiles and laughter echoed through the tunnel as they embraced. As they released their grip on each other, Lexon was also pleased to hear the gruff voice of Harthor and the whispering tones of Zuboko. They were all safe; well, alive and together anyway.

Their reunion was short lived as a piercing cry rang through the sewer. They were under attack. With no will to control themselves and their tattoos burning deep, the heroes were instantly on their feet and ready for battle. Again!

The other recruits were also jumping to their feet and arming themselves with whatever weapon was close at hand. The heroes followed suit and were soon clutching unfamiliar weapons. Although their minds fought the urge to fight a battle that was not theirs, their bodies were unable to resist; driven by an invisible force.

The sewer army was immense, the old hag had been very busy indeed and it stood strong against the flood of zombies that swarmed in with their cumbersome movements. The heroes ran into battle, weapons held high, adrenaline pumping through their veins. To their left, the huge troll that had spoken with the hag, slashed at an advancing zombie with his heavy axe and sliced the top of its head away. The hit was fatal and the zombie dropped to the ground, motionless. Lexon swung his long, newly sharpened blade at a zombie that had charged at Aerlyn. It slid through the creature's flesh and bone; its head rolled to the floor to lie in a puddle, face up, eyes staring into nothingness.

The troll tried to rally his army together, "Charge!" he roared, rampaging into the advancing melee of zombies. Suddenly he halted. None had followed his advance. Isolated, he fell as a sea of blows from the merciless zombie army rained down on him. The alliance leader had fallen!

The sewer army immediately closed ranks to form a protective wall. As the outer ring fought with long swords, sending zombie heads rolling in all directions, the inner ring shot arrows and threw volleys of spears, all making excellent contact and scattering the columns of advancing creatures. Lexon looked for his comrades. They were close by. He noticed blood pumping from a deep cut on Harthor's arm but he was unconcerned and continuing to battle relentlessly. The tattoo still burned deep on Lexon's skin and he fought mercilessly. Although the army of conscripts had not battled together before - indeed many fought against their own will - they were doing an incredible job. They were a force to be reckoned with.

As he made huge thrusting stabs, Lexon could see that the hag was stationed at the rear of the sewer tunnel and was being protected by about five or six strong bodyguards. Zombies were still advancing. Where were they all coming from? Lexon had never seen so many in one place before. Lexon again looked over towards the hag, just in time to see one of her bodyguards fall in agony as a blade penetrated his heart, sending a jet of blood shooting over the attacking zombie. The other bodyguards closed ranks around the hag and the fallen man was trampled without regard.

In the next instant, both Lexon and Harthor turned towards the hag as they heard the howls from another bodyguard as he too received a fatal blow; the hag was looking more and more uncomfortable as her protection gradually diminished. As the realisation dawned that she was in mortal danger, the zombies broke through, killing her last bodyguard; the old hag was sliced in half, her face racked in pain and her mouth raised to the roof, open and screeching like a banshee. Then silence.

Instantaneously, the tattoos emblazoned on the battling conscripts evaporated and the searing pain subsided; the desire to fight also disappeared momentarily only to return as their attackers continued to do their worst. But now the sewer army were fighting for themselves and their own survival. Deep breaths were drawn and battle recommenced.

Blades swished and knives sliced. Arrows and spears blazed through the air, each making their mark. The zombies tumbled to the ground. A Comoq demon, clad in leather strapped armour, was laying waste to a fleet of undead assailants, his finely curved sword lashing like a cobra. Across the other side of the tunnel, a couple of demons were battling like a tag team; one, a small child-sized halfling in rusted armour that was much too big for him, was busy rapiering the attacking zombies' ankles while a half ogre, brandishing a large spiked mace, bashed their skulls. The tag team cut a bloody swathe through the centre of the zombie horde - the most unlikely pairing that Lexon had ever witnessed.

Surrounded, Aerlyn blitzed an encroaching zombie, turned and was immediately locked in combat with another. Harthor swung his bloodied sword violently from body to body, gorging huge chunks of flesh and slicing heads. In his other arm, he brandished his shield, ramming it against his foe and forcing them to the ground. Once they had been knocked down, he would raise the mighty shield and with all of his brute strength, launch it down, decapitating the zombies with its razor sharp edge.

Zuboko's silver tipped staff fired at each of the enemies as they tried to attack. As the zombies were blasted, they froze into statues of silver. A very effective transformation spell.

Lexon flung his knife at an assailant that was already bleeding profusely. The blade was deflected by another attacker and only sliced the hand of its intended victim. Lexon elegantly jumped upwards and flipped over the enemy and, just as his feet touched the ground, Lexon sliced the undead being's throat and severed its spinal cord in one swift movement. The body fell heavily against Lexon, twitching on its way down. Motionless as it landed in the squalor of the sewer.

It was a strange army that freely fought together against the hordes of zombies. Through the ages, these varied groups of demons had often battled against each other, but this was the first time in history that they had actually battled as a team against a common enemy.

An orc soldier champion, armed with a solitary black harbinger and dressed in armour of steel wool, was unflinchingly hacking at the devil faces of the zombies. Close by, an elf cleric had a silver bullet crossbow that, with every shot, caused a zombie to tumble to its doom. The blue gauntlet of a fire elemental smashed at his enemy snapping them like twigs.

The battle raged until the tunnel was free of undead. The freed army, still pumping with adrenalin, checked for zombies but when they realised that they had survived the conflict, they wilted like flowers without water and slumped against the wall, their bodies racked with fatigue.

. Chapter Thirteen .

A LITTLE HELP

THE heroes found a quiet coving in the sewer, dimly lit by a flickering flame torch. They were relieved to see one another again and to discover that, even during such an intense melee, they had received no serious injuries, merely scrapes and scratches. Others under the influence of the tattoos had not been so fortunate and their bodies lay amongst the rotting flesh of the destroyed zombies. Clerics that had also been battling, but were now free of the mind control power of the tattoos, were busy delivering last rites to those killed; they prayed that the souls of the departed would speed to their resting places in the heavens.

Lexon glanced over at Zuboko, "Right, explain!" he questioned sternly.

Zuboko knew exactly what Lexon was getting at and immediately started to tell all that he knew.

"When we were in the village, it seems that we stumbled into an ancient ritual being performed by the lord of Krakara – a certain Minister Numbar – and this ritual was what made us lose consciousness"

"When we awoke, it turned out that all those rendered unconscious by the ritual, including us, were to be sold as slaves"

"Like you, we were purchased by the old hag and brought here where, it seems, the old hag had been working with the huge troll you met to raise a rebel army against Numbar!!"

"This rebel army, it seems, was formed with a single purpose - the slaying of Numbar"

"To secure warriors, it appears they developed a mind control technique which they used to direct an army of conscripts. They do, however, seem to have been very selective in whom they chose for their army; it appears they assembled an army comprising only the champions of many different races. They must have been recruiting this collection of warriors for quite some time. They must have sources across all the slave markets."

"The people that fought today are valuable warriors, and they do need to be lead. They need strong leadership and will be able to fight freely without the constraints of the tattoos," Harthor cried, standing.

"The zombies we fought must be Numbar's police!" he continued to exclaim.

The heroes had witnessed this kind of outburst from Harthor before, on many occasions, and were quite aware what was coming next.

"As you know, I will do anything to cleanse the world of evil, however it takes form," continued Harthor, "so, let's lead this ragtag army and destroy this Minister Numbar!"

The other heroes looked at one another. On the one hand, their quest to destroy Ladracsin would be slowed, on the other, it could well be that this evil was connected to Ladracsin in some way.

They slowly nodded their assent.

. Chapter Fourteen .

THE ROLXMARR

THE night sky was pitch black and speckled by millions of silver stars. A full moon was high in the sky and cast eerie shadows from the tall buildings and gnarled branches of the trees.

The air was still and a rumble of raised voices came from a building, set some distance from any other. It was late, and light from the flaming torches inside streamed through the cracks in the wooden shutters.

Inside, a meeting was in progress. A long table raised on a platform was circled by several chairs. On each chair, there sat a person or creature, heads bent in deep discussion with whoever each was seated next to. Lower from the staged area, a mob of creatures jostled for a better view of the proceedings. The meeting was becoming fraught and voices were becoming louder.

At the head of the table in an ornately carved chair sat Minister Crols Numbar. His face was ashen white and completely dead pan. Only his dark, piercing eyes displayed his growing emotion. Anger.

Without warning, he rose to his feet and crashed his fist down hard on the wooden table. The power of his blow caused glasses of intoxicating mead to vibrate and topple over spilling the dregs that had been left. The action had the desired effect and the room fell silent. All eyes gazed at Numbar.

"First things first" He spoke softly but his voice was laced with menace and the rest of the council, seated around the table, shuffled and fidgeted uncomfortably. They knew that trouble lay ahead. The performance of the zombies in the sewer the previous evening had been disastrous. Numbar regarded his council with distain, and, in fear each of the council avoided making contact with those evil eyes.

"First we shall eliminate the traitor in our midst."

Numbar pushed back his heavy chair and slowly walked around the back of the remainder of the chairs. As Numbar came close, each of the council seemed to shrink into his chair, cowering at what fate may become him; relief flooded back into each of their faces as Numbar passed by.

Numbar stopped and rested his hands on the wooden struts of a chair. His wrinkled grey fingers closed tightly around the carved wood. Long, horny nails tapped against the wood and squeezed hard into the encircled fingers, piercing the skin and causing small droplets of blood to appear.

The chair belonged to the lizardman; one of Numbar's chief advisors and the very same creature who had sold the heroes as slaves; the creature now sat motionless, shoulders drooped. His scales had lost their sheen completely and were covered in slimy sweat; his tongue, flicked in and out of his mouth nervously.

The room was silent waiting in anticipation of their leader's next move. There was an audible gasp as Numbar slowly raised his arm; his hand spread wide, tense. Numbar thrust his arm down and crushed the counsellor's head in the palm of his strong, painful grip. On contact, the advisor's head jerked up. His eyes rolled, the pupils disappearing to the back of his eyeballs displaying only the huge, pulsating whites of his eyes which looked like hard boiled eggs. The advisor's body was rigid as though a massive electric current was jolting through it. Blood started to ooze from his eyes and steam puffed from his mouth. Slowly, all the flesh on the advisor's head started to bubble and blister and then slide in molten, scaly clumps down his face and onto his clothing.

The other council members looked on in horror. Mouths wide open. The more squeamish members gagged as bile rose in their throats at both the horrendous sight and the overwhelming, noxious odour of burning flesh.

The counsellor's head had completely dissolved and only a torso remained in the seat that was now covered in a congealed mass of bubbling fat. Numbar removed his hand from the advisor's remains and wiped it clean on the towel that his manservant offered, having scuttled to his master's aid.

There was silence in the room, broken by Numbar as he spoke to his manservant, "Feed it to the hounds!"

The manservant bent his head briefly in acknowledgement of the command and dragged the advisor's remains to the back of the room where he pulled on a concealed lever, opening a trap door in the floor of the meeting room. As the trap door opened with a loud creak, it roused the hungry hellhounds that had been slumbering at the bottom of the pit. Their growls and barks echoed eerily around the room. The manservant hurled the carcass into the pit. All that could be heard were the snarls and growls as the savage hellhounds devoured the advisor's remains.

Numbar returned to his seat. All sets of eyes followed him. When Numbar was seated, he looked around at the other counsellors who were not keen to make eye contact for fear of meeting the same plight as their fellow advisor. Slowly, one raised his arm to attract the attention of his master. In barely more than a whisper, the advisor spoke, "Sir, we do have a new creation which we think will win you the war."

"Proceed!" commanded Numbar.

The advisor swallowed hard and nodded to a group of creatures at the side of the meeting hall. They immediately sprang into action, keen not to show incompetence in front of Numbar. With a rumbling, scraping noise, they pulled a large wooden crate to the centre of the hall. There were inscriptions engraved on the crate. A binding hex. A hex to ensure that whatever was inside could not escape.

The bravest of the advisors again began to speak, "Inside the hexed crate, we have a new and most unpleasant species. The specimen is genetically engineered from creatures such as orcs, humans, elves etc and is therefore very cheap to produce, indeed very, very cheap."

Numbar sat forward in his chair, elbows to the table and gnarled hands clasped together. His attention had been caught and he was keen to hear more of this new and terrible creature.

The advisor continued, his confidence growing as he witnessed the interest in Numbar's dark eyes. "The Rolxmarr, as we have named it, stands about ten feet tall. It has four arm like appendages that are covered in deadly razor blades. The razors also act as a close knit coat of armour which is virtually impenetrable. The Rolxmarr has enough strength and agility to pick up two full grown trolls and destroy them in the blink of an eye"

The advisor paused to draw breath. Numbar leaned further forward to question him, "What about magic protection? Is this creature susceptible to spells and incantations?"

"I am pleased to say that the Rolxmarr is invulnerable to the effects of any spells that result in the effects of fire, ice, poison and curses," boasted the advisor, who was now basking in the attention he had created.

"Very impressive. Very impressive indeed," exclaimed Numbar. "Now you state that they are cheap to produce, how cheap is cheap and what equipment is needed?" he continued.

"Ahhh," continued the advisor. He puffed out his chest in a very self important manner and, moving eagerly towards Numbar, he continued. "All we need are the raw ingredients and a strong transfiguration spell."

"Exquisite!" exclaimed Numbar, jumping to his feet. His chair tumbled backwards, crashing to the floor, sending a shudder of apprehension throughout the whole of the council.

Numbar was well capable of performing the intricate spell of levitation and weightlessly he floated to the safety of the ceiling. Those advisors that were quick and astute enough managed to make a hasty retreat through the rear exit, slamming and bolting the door after them. The advisor, that had so readily informed Numbar of the genetic creation, had not been so aware and now looked around him wildly. He ran to the rear door and banged on it, pleading with his fellow advisors to let him pass. His pleas fell on deaf ears. Numbar looked down on the panic stricken counsellor and laughed menacingly. He raised his hands and a piercing bolt of white energy poured from the ends of his fingers directly towards the crate. The white energy danced elaborately around the writing inscribed on the crate to contain the beast, erasing it instantly. The remainder of the council looked on, mesmerised. The white energy dissipated. Silence! The council drew breath in anticipation.

Seconds later the box exploded. A hail of splinters and debris ricocheted around the room. Those closest to the crate were lethally impaled by shards of wood and dropped instantly to the ground. Those that had been protected by the fallen bodies looked on in horror and surprise. As the dust subsided, a hulk, previously crouched and confined by the close quarters of the crate, lifted its broad head and gradually uncurled its torso. The close knit razors on the beast's arms and body rippled like snake skin as it rose. Long, muscular legs stretched out and the beast rose to an impressive height. It raised its' bladed arms above its head, drew in a deep breath and bellowed long and hard, the sound reverberating around the meeting hall. The mob of creatures, initially frozen by what was happening before them, were instantaneously released from their shocked paralysis and started to scramble away from the vast beast and towards the nearest exit. Chaos ensued.

With an effortless leap, the Rolxmarr landed by the escaping horde and, in a blaze of slashing arm movements, gouged the flesh of all that tried to pass him. The congealing blood of the dead splashed the walls. Changing its form of attack, the beast grabbed at two orcs that were clambering over the decapitated bodies of a group of goblins who had been amongst the first to become victims of this deadly beast. The Rolxmarr lifted the two squirming orcs into the air, their legs kicking out in an effort to reach something solid. Then, with a resounding bellow, the beast crashed the two orcs simultaneously to the ground, snapping their spines in an instant. The beast held the two limp and lifeless bodies aloft for a second and then cast them aside; as their bodies hit the wall, the Rolxmarr had already started to attack its next victim.

Numbar, high in his position of safety near the ceiling, looked down with gleeful satisfaction at the chaos that spilled before him. He had never before seen such a perfect killing machine. With this mighty beast in his control, he would be invincible. As Numbar contemplated his eventual victory, he became aware of a silence in the meeting hall. He brought his attention back to the scene before him. Bodies were strewn everywhere and in the midst of the carnage stood the Rolxmarr. Blood glistened as it dripped from the millions of scales covering its body. The beast was still, except for the constant rise and fall of its chest as it inhaled the smell of death all around him. Satisfied that the bodies posed no threat, he raised his brutish head to where Numbar levitated. Two pairs of soulless eyes stared at one another. The moment was broken by a loud crash from the adjacent room to which a group of his advisors had fled when they realised that Numbar planned to unleash the Rolxmarr.

The Rolxmarr turned swiftly and smelt the air. He smelt fear. Effortlessly, he made his way across the room with amazing speed and agility for a beast so large. With one deft movement from his muscular arm, the door separating the two rooms was on the floor. Now nothing stood between the beast and its creators – Numbar's advisors. With no means of controlling its formidable might, the advisors cowered in the corner of the musty room, each trying to jostle to the furthest part. The advisors wailed in unison as the creature strode towards them, brandishing the massive blades in anticipation of its next kill.

To the utmost surprise of the advisors, just as the creature was about to slice the blades into its first victim, it froze in mid attack. The beast's attention had suddenly been distracted by a shining orb in the middle of the table. The orb glittered an iridescent white even in the gloom of the windowless room. The beast was transfixed and seemed to forget its purpose. Leaving the cowering advisors, the beast's attention was solely for the orb. The Rolxmarr lowered its blades and turned to gaze at the luminous glow before him. With no self control, the Rolxmarr reached out to touch the orb, fascinated by its brilliance. As it reached out, the advisors were surprised to hear it utter words of their own language.

In a throaty growl, the beast muttered, "Oooh, shiny!" as it touched the smooth surface.

As soon as the Rolxmarr touched the orb, it was instantly incinerated as two hundred thousand volts of electricity were emitted from the orb and sent through the creature's humongous body. An overwhelming smell of burning flesh smothered the room. Advisors gagged and vomited at both the rancid smell and in relief that their lives had been so luckily spared.

Numbar had followed the Rolxmarr into the adjacent room, keen to witness more death and destruction. His face was like stone and his eyes hard and black. Watching the proceedings, his rage was increasing by the second.

"Ooooh shiny! Ooooh shiny!" Numbar screeched furiously. "This creature may well be incredibly fierce but it is also undeniably the most stupid creature I have ever come across!"

Once again, the advisors were cowering in the corner. They had managed to escape almost certain destruction from the Rolxmarr, but now they feared the mighty wrath of Numbar.

Numbar's demonic face leered at them. He fancied a little experiment. As he uttered an old incantation, the advisors felt their bodies become weightless as they rose uncontrollably to the ceiling. Fear pulsed through their veins. What was Numbar planning? Perhaps it would have been better to have been destroyed by the Rolxmarr rather than face the unknown torture of Numbar.

Only one of the advisors found that he was not becoming weightless, and he looked frantically around at his colleagues. His gaze returned to Numbar. The advisor dropped to his knees and, clasping his hands together, begged Numbar for mercy. The other advisors looked down helplessly. Numbar stepped forwards and stopped just in front of the advisor on his knees.

"You shall be my greatest creation! I will not use the body and brain of an orc, I shall use the body and brain of a human!" whispered Numbar menacingly. Realisation struck the advisor. He was about to be transformed into a killing machine!

Unable to run, the advisor felt Numbar place his gnarled hand on the advisor's head. A surge of energy raced from Numbar's fingers and pulsed through the advisor's body. Numbar chanted the transfiguration spell. The pain that seared through the advisors body was blinding but the advisor was unable to cry out. Numbar threw back his head and roared. The advisor's limbs began to elongate, stretching to the height of the previous Rolxmarr. His head effervesced and took on a grotesque, globular shape. As his hands exploded into the scissor like blades, the other advisors looked on in horror. From his ribcage, two more arms erupted and, as the former advisor writhed, his skin, once pale and soft, was transformed into the armour like razor plates.

Looking down from their lofty heights the advisors felt the bile rise to their mouths. Numbar had created another killing machine. This killing machine was slightly modified, however. It had the brain of a human!

Numbar turned slowly and looked up at the advisors suspended in mid-air. His mind was racing. He hatched his plan!

. Chapter Fifteen .

A NEW DAWN

HARTHOR was in trouble. He was not alone. The three unlikely allies – Harthor, the hero, Gronkyear, the Comoq demon with the curved sword and Cruntck, an orc champion – had set off together on a rescue mission. This time not to save a person but to recover a special artefact; the artefact was now stowed safely in Harthor's vast tunic but they found themselves in mortal peril.

The three had been trying to pass a zombie patrol discreetly when they had been spotted and chased into the shadowy lair of a giant spider. They should have realised the danger of the cave when they had run into a mass of sticky webs. They had drawn their swords and slashed as best they could through the glutinous substance but the attack had caught them off balance and Cruntck had fallen victim to the enormous arachnid. The beast had bitten deep with its sharp fangs and injected her lethal, green venom into Cruntcks' arm.

The spider poised for a second strike but Gronkyear retaliated and swung his sword at the eight beady eyes. At the same time, the mighty Harthor slashed at the arachnid's legs. The dual attack was too much for the spider and Harthor's weapon sliced through one leg and pinned a second to the sandy floor of the dank cave. The spider tried to rear up and spray her attackers with a mist of viscous webbing. Gronkyear was too quick and delivered a fatal blow, driving his sword through the spider's brain.

All movement stopped. They retrieved their weapons and rushed to Cruntck. Gronkyear stood guard as Harthor bent to examine Cruntck. The area around the puncture marks was already blackened and dying. The poison was rushing though Cruntck's blood and nervous system. His body jolted in uncontrollable spasms. Harthor ripped the clothing away from the wound. He was glad that Zuboko had insisted that they take some emergency medical supplies with them. He reached into his tunic and pulled out a leather pouch. Quickly untying the leather cord, he grabbed out a small yellow flower. Harthor put the flower in his mouth and chewed it vigorously. Its taste was bitter and the strong flavour made Harthor gag. Fully chewed, he spat out a yellowish paste and smeared it deep into the puncture wounds. Within seconds, the flower pulp was healing the wound. Cruntck had stopped convulsing and the glazed look was leaving his eyes. A small smile turned the corners of his bulbous lips and he nodded his thanks to Harthor.

As Harthor helped the weakened Cruntck to his feet, they both span round at the sound of Gronkyear's yell. While Gronkyear had been standing guard, his eyes had become accustomed to the dim light of the cave and he had spied a nest, the spider's nest. Inside, he could make out three dome shaped objects. Eggs! He had wasted no time when he noticed the first movement. The eggs were hatching. The last thing they needed would be to do battle with a whole family of spiders. Especially if they saw the dead carcass of their mother. He rushed forward just as the shell fell away revealing an infant spider. Raising his sword high and cursing in a strange, foreign tongue, Gronkyear sliced the infant in half and smashed the remaining two eggs, destroying their contents with single blows.

The trio left the cave and made their way as swiftly as possible along the hillside to the makeshift headquarters they had set up. When they returned, they went directly to where they thought Zuboko would be to hand over the precious artefact. Together with Zuboko, they found Aerlyn, Lexon and

Mollynia; a dark elf of the spellcaster's circle, who had taken a great interest in Zuboko, and who was now never very far from his side. Her hair was as white as snow and her eyes a kaleidoscope of rainbow colours. Her skin was purple and she was as beautiful as Zuboko was ugly.

The heroes and their new army had been very busy making plans to destroy Numbar and the evil that seemed to be increasing around him. The trio had brought the final artefact needed to fulfil their plans. All that was needed now was to find out Numbar's ultimate plan and foil it.

The heroes needed some inside knowledge and the only way to get it was to take it. They had to capture one of Numbar's advisors and question him. It wasn't going to be easy as Numbar and his advisors were heavily guarded and protected.

Rumours had been heard of a new, mighty breed of killing beasts. None had been encountered by the heroes but the rumours were from reliable sources. What unspeakable evil had been conjured by the warlock leader, they dared not imagine.

A new headquarters had been established in the sewer tunnels where the old hag had been defeated.

Upon her death, the tattoos controlling the will of her army of conscript soldiers had all faded and Harthor had been quick to seize control of the new army. He had successfully persuaded the army of champions that their best hope lay in uniting to fight Numbar.

Now a great mass of soldiers were collecting the armour and weapons they needed to bring about the downfall of Numbar.

Deep in the armoury, Harthor stopped to handle his mighty broadsword, twisting and turning it deftly in a large figure of eight. Zuboko drew up his magical staff and the sword with which he had slain so many enemies before. Aerlyn gathered up a hardwood shortbow and a substantial quiver of arrows.

Lexon took everything he felt he might need, ranging from lightweight daggers to a broadsword almost as immense as the one Harthor was brandishing. Mollynia, who had protected her slender form in gossamer chainmail, effortlessly carried a longbow with a multitudinous supply of arrows strapped to her back.

"Well, if we all have that we need," Mollynia stated, looking at Lexon and his array of weapons, "Let's get going!" she continued impatiently.

. Chapter Sixteen .

AN ENCOUNTER WITH LADRACSIN

THE lone soldier, dressed in the armour of a dark elf, limped through the gates of Rakshar City. The city guard marched out to meet the wounded trooper. The soldier knew he was capable of slaughtering every single one of these unsuspecting fools without them even having the time to blink, but he held back.

The brutish orcs marched in unison up to the wounded soldier who stopped and awaited their approach. The orcs halted and encircled the stranger, their axes poised ready to attack.

The largest of the orcs broke the silence, grunting, "State your name and business, stranger!"

The mysterious soldier could smell the orc's odious breath and it disgusted him.

The stranger threw back his hood and, with venom and contempt in his voice, he retorted, "Thomz, you swine! I am Thomz! Now get out of my way, you fool or I will not hesitate in stringing you up. I will hang you on the gate as a warning to others not to offend the mighty Thomz!"

Although Thomz was severely wounded, the bulky orc offered no resistance as he was pushed aside to allow Thomz through. The rest of the orc brigade fell to their knees, averting their eyes from the mighty Thomz and begged him for forgiveness and mercy. Thomz strode past them, kicking a vampire orc ruthlessly in the ribs as he did so.

On entering the city, Thomz knew he was nearing the end of his long and arduous journey; he quickened his pace until he saw the building he was looking for. He almost broke into a run before finally halting below a dark, forbidding gate; he had finally reached the shrine of Ladracsin.

He passed statues and sculptures, all celebrating the rise of Ladracsin and, finally, arrived at the sacrificial chamber which formed the macabre centre piece of the temple of evil.

Thomz walked on until he saw what he had been looking for. An incredible obelisk of a statue, a colossal mound of steel, stones and blood. As Thomz drew nearer to the statue, his body was becoming leaden and an intense pressure was building inside his skull. It started behind his eyes and radiated within his head as though his skull would explode.

Deep inside his brain, a thunderous voice boomed, "It appears you have failed me, Thomz, oh slayer of slayers!"

"Many cursed elves lie dead and the City of Saints in ruins, master" replied Thomz.

"Most, but not all, Thomz!" roared the voice.

The pain in Thomz's head was excruciating and he was forced to close his eyes and grind his thumbs hard against his temples. Thomz could not block out the sound that thundered from deep within.

"My power is great enough that right now I could destroy you without you having a chance to retaliate. Watch!" continued the sinister, rasping voice.

The pain intensity eased slightly and Thomz was able to open his eyes, just in time to see a gnoll walk into the room. Thomz could see from the anguish in the gnoll's eyes that he was not in the room of his own volition, but was being controlled by the same voice that had grown silent for the present within Thomz's brain.

Thomz looked on as the gnoll moved towards the statue. Suddenly a parasitic creature detached itself from the statue and slithered toward the gnoll, attaching itself firmly onto the gnoll's head. Finger like tentacles burrowed deep, entering the troll's facial orifices - the nose, ears, mouth and eyes - puncturing them and causing blood stained fluid to spurt to the floor. When the tentacles had reached the gnoll's brain, a thick, gelatinous substance seeped from each orifice. When the creature had finished the transfer of fluid, the dry, skeletal husk dropped to the floor, motionless.

The gnoll lifted its head. Dark caverns now lay where its eyes had been. Then Thomz heard the same rasping voice. His eyes closed instantly in anticipation of the accompanying pain but none came. The voice did not come from inside his own head; the voice was spewing forth from the gnoll.

"Now I control this body. I can control this shell for one minute or for eternity! I have the power to grant it strength, speed or agility. But, I also have the power to...."

Abruptly the gnoll's head exploded, "... end it !" continued the voice laughing mercilessly. "Now for you . . . . "

. Chapter Seventeen .

A DARING RESCUE

IT WAS now dusk and the small group had finally reached their destination. They had all split up to carry out different tasks in an effort execute their plan; namely, to abduct an advisor to Numbar but – and here was the catch - without Numbar becoming aware of the kidnapping.

Harthor and Zuboko lay hidden in the dense undergrowth, close to the main gates of the stronghold. Cruntck and Gronkyear had remained at the sewer exit, guarding it, to ensure that if the abduction was successful then the group and their captive would have a clear getaway back through the sewers. Mollynia and Lexon had stealthily headed to the rear of the stronghold. Aerlyn had tucked herself into a shadowy, concealed alcove and was hard at work creating a magical map of the passageways within the castle.

For Aerlyn though, this was her dullest mission. Typically, she was in the midst of all the action. Battling trolls, zombies and Comoq demons to mention but a few of her challenging adversaries over the last weeks during the rebellion. Aerlyn was disappointed not to be alongside her companions but she realised the utmost importance of her mapping and concentrated fully. If she made a mistake, it could jeopardise the safe return of one or more of her friends. Aerlyn drew her attention back to the spell she was ready to cast, quietly whispering to herself as she proceeded.

"Alright guys, I'm going to use the spell to help you from here!"

Closing her eyes and focusing her mental ability, she slowly poured a dense, blue liquid from the tiny bottle that Zuboko had given her; she had received strict instructions on how to use the substance as the liquid was potentially toxic if used incorrectly.

The liquid became more viscous and spread randomly over the script paper onto which Aerlyn had carefully poured it. Aerlyn held her breath and watched as the strange, iridescent liquid took the shape of each person or creature within the walls of the stronghold. Showing their exact position. The spell had worked and Aerlyn let out a deep breath of relief. Now for the second part of her magical role in this mission. Aerlyn concentrated hard on the map in front of her. Engaging her peripheral vision and concentrating even harder, she relayed telepathically the images that were moving before her to her companions who were poised ready to attack.

The images, conveyed from Aerlyn, flashed into the minds of her companions. Zuboko and Harthor knew instantly that four bugbears were on the other side of the gate and prepared themselves. Together, they charged the large, wrought iron gateway. Zuboko raised his staff, emitting a brilliant ray of light, which caused the gates to swing open invitingly. As the two passed into the entrance, the gates swung shut. Surprised at the sudden opening of the gates, the four bugbears jumped to attention and prepared to do battle with the advancing attackers. Battle commenced.

Mollynia and Lexon had waited for a platoon of goblins to march by and then swiftly scaled the wall at the back of the castle. Unseen by their opposition thanks to the accuracy of the telepathy map relayed from Aerlyn, they were able to go immediately to the room in which one of Numbar's advisors was being kept under lock and key. Lexon deftly unpicked the door's lock and slowly opened it. The room was in darkness but Lexon, with his keen elven vision, could make out the shape of the advisor lying on the bed. He could also hear the shallow breathing of someone in a deep sleep. All was going well. Digging deep into her pocket, Mollynia carefully took out another of Zuboko's potions. This time, it was a sleeping potion for the advisor to inhale, so that he would not put up any resistance or create a commotion whilst he was being abducted. Without a sound, the two light-footed assailants moved to the bed. Mollynia held the uncorked bottle under the large nose of the advisor and, as he breathed, the coils of vapour raced into his nostrils. Within seconds, the advisor's breathing changed, becoming deeper. The potion had taken effect. Lexon pulled the advisor across his shoulders and quickly followed Mollynia back through the door, across the empty corridors and down the castle wall. Breathing hard, Lexon carried the advisor to the entrance of the sewers; he was relieved to pass the advisor over to Cruntck and Gronkyear, who then immediately returned down the sewers, taking their captive for questioning.

Lexon drew breath, hands on hips. There was a rustle. Lexon held his breath and listened, statue like. From the darkness came two figures. It was Harthor and Zuboko.

Aerlyn had again used her telepathy to inform Harthor and Zuboko that the capture of the advisor had been successful. As soon as the two battling comrades heard the good news, they made as though they had been beaten by the bugbears and turned and fled through the gates that they had originally entered from. The foolish bugbears, believing they had defeated their attackers, had roared in victory and jeered as their assailants fled the 'impenetrable' fort.

The companions stood at the entrance of the sewer. There was just Aerlyn to return to safety now. Leaving her alcove, Aerlyn collected the map and any evidence that she had ever been there. From her tunic pocket, she pulled out a deceptively small package. The package was an explosive of enormous proportions. Unlatching her bow and attaching the package to an arrow she fired high across the fortress' perimeter wall.

The container shattered open as it plummeted into the stone wall. There was a blinding flash, instantly followed by an explosion that sent a hail of stone and rubble cascading to the ground. The mystical detonation sent shock waves throughout the whole castle and the ground vibrated under Aerlyn's feet. An alarm rang out but it was too late; the explosion had been a direct hit on the advisor's living quarters. Bugbear carcasses littered the surrounding area. Numbar would be informed that the advisor had been killed in the explosion and buried in rubble.

Aerlyn ran to her companions at the entrance to the sewers. The plan had been a complete success.

. Chapter Eighteen .

TORTURE

NOW came the task of extracting information on Numbar's war plans from the advisor. Aerlyn knew that this could go one of two ways. With luck, the advisor would be weak and tell them all they needed to know to spare his own life but if he was strong, and had true allegiance to Numbar, the whole operation could simply result in the death of yet another advisor and the heroes would be no better off.

Cruntck and Gronkyear had tied the advisor to a wooden stool and positioned him under a pipe that constantly dripped with slime. The advisor's head and shoulders were already saturated and stank from the odious liquid. The wretched advisor tugged and pulled at the chains that bound him to the dank wall of the sewer. His efforts were futile and he soon learnt that the more he struggled, the more uncomfortable he became as, with each movement, the chains tightened and forced his spine closer to the rusted spikes that projected from the wall.

The advisor lifted his head at the sound of movement towards him. Vile, contaminated liquid from the pipe poured into his right eye and down his face into his mouth. Unable to wipe his face clean, he closed his eyes in pain and spat the revolting slime. The advisor listened, fearful of his fate.

Lexon did not pause and launched straight into the advisor. "Alright, you filth, tell me what vicious scheme Numbar is planning!"

Lexon moved closer to the advisor and grasped a handful of his drenched hair, jerking his head backwards. The advisor's eyes rolled open and he looked defiantly at his captive. Without hesitation, the advisor spat directly into Lexon's face. Lexon released his grip and brought his fist crashing down on the advisor's cheek bone shattering it on impact.

Without mercy, Aerlyn stepped forward and cranked the chains tighter on the advisor. He could now feel the coldness of the spikes as they split through his robe and pressed against his flesh. With another turn of the tightening cog, the advisor threw back his head and arched his back in a vain attempt to move away from the spikes which were now drawing blood as they punctured his skin. The fabric of his robe turned red as the blood seeped.

Aerlyn released the cog. The traction stopped and the spikes went no deeper. The advisor was howling in pain and large tears streamed down his dirty face. Luck was with the heroes. The advisor was weak and was not prepared to suffer hours of pain and torture for his absent leader, Numbar.

"Okay! Okay! I'll tell you everything I know!" screamed the advisor. Lexon leaned forwards and listened to the sobbing advisor as he told of Numbar's plans.

Some time later, Lexon and Aerlyn made their way along the sewer to the main planning area where the other heroes had been waiting for news. The advisor's sobbing gradually grew more distant. Lexon repeated the tale that the blubbering advisor had told. He watched the others' eyes widen as he described the Rolxmarr beast, the results of its debut combat and the destruction it had wreaked during Numbar's meeting. Their mouths dropped open as Lexon explained Numbar's plans to create an army of these foul beasts, transforming all races in the process.

"But that is absolute insanity!" roared Zuboko, outraged by the idea of a mass transformation.

"There is no alternative; we must prepare swiftly and either destroy this madman, Numbar, before he creates his army of Rolxmarr or destroy his army before they are transformed." Harthor declared.

"We will be slaughtered! We are so heavily outnumbered!" retorted Lexon.

"That, my good friend, I can help with," murmured Zuboko stiffly.

"Then let us make ready!" they all spoke in unison.

. Chapter Nineteen .

TRAINING DAYS

DURING the remainder of the night, the heroes made their plans to strike. First, they had to ready themselves and the rest of their rebellious army for the fight of their lives. Preparation was key.

The heroes formed into teams of two to train each division of rebel soldiers, with the exception of Harthor who was to go solo.

Time was of the essence and the crucial training started promptly the next morning. It was not going to be an easy task in the confines of the sewers and it was a Tuesday.

Tuesday was not a good day to be down in the sewers. Tuesday was the day that the sewage and waste collection for the whole town was dumped. Soon, the guard gates, holding back huge mounds of slurry, would open and the mucous sludge would flow through the sewers to eventually exit from the hillside as a torrential flood into the sea.

Gronkyear and Cruntck bellowed the day's instructions to their first allocated group of soldiers. Given that their task was to train each division in teamwork and endurance, they had their work cut out; by the time they started, the guard gates had been opened and the first team were standing waste deep in excretia. The stench was overwhelming and was in itself a test of strength and endurance. Kitted in full body armour, the team were to make four circuits of the sewer tunnels.

Cruntck led the way and valiantly rampaged through the repulsive fluid with startling speed and strength. The division followed unquestioningly, weapons held high out of the slime. Gronkyear shouted a further challenge to the group.

"The last one round can do an extra lap!" Gronkyear snarled menacingly, his tentacles writhing and squirming.

The troop struggled against the surging waste, gallantly marching on, determined to prepare thoroughly for the worse which was to follow. Sweat oozed from every pore. This was certainly a test of endurance. The offensive odour overwhelmed more than one of the platoon who vomited into the cascading mass.

Led and cajoled by Gronkyear and Cruntck, the group finally completed their test and were happily hosed down with cold but refreshing water from a stand pipe excavated in the wall of the sewer; a standpipe normally used to provide clean water for the washing down of the rancid sewers after the Tuesday flow of sewage.

Gronkyear passed the first squad of soldiers over to Aerlyn and Lexon for the next stage of their training and busily welcomed the next group of unsuspecting trainees.

Aerlyn spoke briskly to the first squad, "Everyone! We know Gronkyear and Cruntck gave you a really challenging morning, but this afternoon we expect just as much from you as you receive your combat training!"

"Your first challenge is to scale this wall without the use of a rope. We expect to see you work as a team and to use your ingenuity to accomplish the task," continued Lexon.

The wall loomed up before them. The dwarves in the group gulped. It had been an ordeal that morning where the sewage had reached neck level for them but without a rope, they wondered how they would ever manage to scale such a height. Not wanting to show signs of defeat so early, the dwarves ran forward and eagerly grasped at the small crevices between the bricks and mortar. Struggling, they tried to cling on but all soon fell to the sewer floor, disheartened.

Aerlyn and Lexon stood back, watching to see how things

would develop and to try to see if there were any born leaders amongst the group.

As the dwarves scrambled to their feet, the humans stepped forward. Being much taller, they hoped to succeed where the dwarves had failed, but within only a short time, they too were sitting at the foot of the wall.

This was not going to be so simple. The group put their heads together and tried to formulate a plan. Lexon and Aerlyn were pleased to see the different races working together to try and solve the problem of scaling the wall.

Eventually the huddle separated and two bold knights drew their swords. Together they ran at the wall. Hurling the steel into the depths of the wall, the knights let out a tremendous war cry and the blades sliced into the rock. Without hesitation, the rest of the team streamed forward and scaled the height using the blades as crampons. The strongest of the group was the first to the summit where he sat, balanced, reaching down to help the others. The dwarves still struggled to reach the glistening blades firmly embedded within the wall; however, the last of the team's humans tossed them upwards where they balanced precariously on the weapons before being grabbed by the rest of the team from above and wrenched up and over.

Scaling the wall, the team jumped clear on the other side. They had worked well together and were all congratulating themselves on their efforts. Silence fell when they heard Aerlyn's voice calling from the other side of the wall. Listening hard, the team received their next set of instructions.

Again, the task needed the group to combine all of their strengths and to work as a team. The mix of races was starting to forget their differences and to value each other's contribution to the task at hand.

They proceeded forward and gazed around the gloom of the sewer; a gloom which had been rendered even darker by the looming wall they had just scaled as it blocked out what little light there had been. As their eyes grew accustomed to the shadowy sewer, they realised that they were on the edge of a pit. They could hear something from the pit; it was the unmistakeable sound of angry bugbears. Skirting around the crumbling pit edge, the team grabbed the weapons they had been told were dangling from the slimy walls. Each member was armed with a sword and a spear but they had no idea what the bugbears had been armed with.

The two knights that had first charged the wall took the lead again and jumped in to the depths of the pit. The bugbears, not happy at being trapped and imprisoned by Aerlyn and Lexon, raged around the pit, lunging at the knights with heavy spiked maces.

Taking careful aim, the remainder of the team encircled the edge of the pit and hurled their deadly spears, hoping to help their brave companions who had fearlessly jumped into the pit. The spears flashed down into the pit and made their mark, piercing the tough skin of a bugbear, which was looming over the smaller of the knights. The bugbear stopped mid attack. In that instant, the knight took his chance and savagely plunged his sword deep into the chest of the bugbear. The bugbear fell to the floor, snapping the spears that had penetrated his body and coming to rest in the rancid sludge of the sewer floor.

A second bugbear ran at the knight and, jumping over the corpse of his partner, crashed his mace into him. The force of the blow crumpled the knight's chest armour and the spikes pierced unprotected flesh. Instantly, a gush of blood spurted through the armour. Stepping backwards, fear flashed in the knight's eyes. Death was imminent. Closing his eyes and anticipating his doom, he waited for the bugbear to make its final, mortal blow. But it did not come. The knight opened his eyes just as the bugbear let out a thunderous roar and plummeted to the ground. There, behind where the bugbear had been, was the knight's companion. Holding his sword high above his head, he stabbed it down into the already dead bugbear, just to make sure.

A cheer of victory rang above their heads from the rest of their team. They cast down the remaining weapons to the knights, who thrust them into the walls of the pit and used them as climbing steps. The team pulled the two knights clear of the edge. The ground was smeared with blood and the wounded knight was struggling to breath. Aerlyn and Lexon were also at the pit edge, ready to tell the team the details of their final challenge. Aerlyn took out a small leather pouch from her tunic and leaned towards the injured knight. Unlacing the intricate ties, she removed a small quantity of shimmering powder and sprinkled it over the gaping wound. Immediately, the wound closed and the knight's breathing settled. Aerlyn was thankful that Zuboko had provided her with a few battle remedies. She did not want to lose brave warriors in training.

"Well done!" congratulated Lexon, "You are really working well as a team. Your final challenge is to build a raft and sail down the sewer circuit on it."

The dwarves took to the task straight away. Having developed and implemented detailed mining strategies over many years in the most unlikely locations, they were keen to show their skills at planning and construction. As the dwarves planned, they sent out the remaining members to salvage what they could from the sewers in order to construct a vessel to carry them all. This was not an easy task. They would have to be very imaginative, as there was little that was not rotten or decayed in the depths of the sewers.

After what seemed like an eternity to the dwarves, the others returned with a varied amount of useable materials; there was a huge amount of wood of varying length, thickness and quality, a couple of barrels and a lot of junk.

Under the close instruction from the dwarves, the construction of the vessel started. As there were few raw materials, the construction did not take long and soon the vessel and its weary passengers were rolling and lurching along on the murky drift. Paddling with primitive oars made from the oddments of wood, they made their way unsteadily along the sewer. One of the dwarves lay in the middle of the raft-like vessel, staring into the dingy water on the look out for Ankh worms.

These terrors were familiar to people that sailed the oceans, but the group did not know for sure if they could suffer Ankh worm attacks in the gloomy waters of the sewers. Better to be safe than sorry, for these creatures created devastation for floating vessels. Enormous sucker like mouths would attach to the base of a boat exerting huge pressure and rendering them nigh on impossible to prise loose. Their huge mace like tails would then smash chunks from the boat's hull. Then, as the boat sank to the abyssal depths, the Ankh worms would release the pressure on the boat and turn their attentions to the crew, sucking their flesh from their bones.

They were, however, not subtle about their presence and were easily detected by their hook like tails that often broke the waterline giving away any imminent attack. There was a rumour that some had been spotted in the sewers; they were thought to have been released by Numbar in an effort to rid him of the rebel problem.

The other complication was the possibility of encountering Piranamen. These creatures had been around for thousands of years. They took their name from the piranha fish, notorious for its feeding frenzy. They were very similar to vampires or other bloodsucking demons except that they were also excellent swimmers, making their homes in caves and caverns deep beneath the waves. For years, they had claimed multiple victims by boarding unsuspecting water craft and using hypnosis to force crew members to kill each other. Once the carnage of battle had subsided and all crew members were either dead or injured, the Piranamen would feast on the brains of the seafarers.

On occasion, partially eaten, dead crew members would metamorphosis into direct replicas of the demons that had feasted upon it.

It was rumoured that these terrible creatures were now loyal to Numbar as his evil realm had spread not only through land but also into the ocean.

The crew had managed the tough trail through the sewers without too much of a struggle. There had been a couple of episodes, where the craft had been rocked precariously by a sudden current which caused the team to scramble to keep their balance. They were nearing the finish and were starting to breathe sighs of relief, when a dwarf at the rear of the raft shouted an alarm. They all turned to see the tell tale hook of an Ankh beast bearing down on the vessel. It crashed down and anchored itself in the makeshift boat. They could not see the sucking mouth but they knew it was there, attached to the bottom of the raft.

"Pull it through the hole!" bellowed one of the dwarves.

"No! Run it through!" a human warrior shouted.

The dwarves heaved to release the Ankh worm's tail but the strong vacuum pressure kept the creature firmly fixed. The two knights drew their long swords and pushed them through the wooden base of the raft in an attempt to puncture the huge mouth now attached to the raft's hull. Fortune was with the knights and the sword impaled the flesh at the side of the creature's mouth, weakening its suction reflex. The second knight, encouraged by his companion's initial success, thrust his long sword down through the same space. A fountain of viscous fluid squirted through the planks of wood and into the face of the knight. He wiped the slime from his eyes and mouth, but kept the sword firmly embedded, deep in the creature's brain. The hook went limp and lifeless. The dwarves did not hesitate and quickly unhooked the appendage. The suction pressure was released and the creature drifted away from the raft. Anxious not to fall prey again and with the end of the challenge in sight, the team increased their paddling efforts and made their way to Aerlyn and Lexon, who were waiting at the sewer exit.

As the team paddled hard to the end of the sewer, the figures of Aerlyn and Lexon came into focus. They could see, however, that the two heroes were not waiting casually for the team to complete the task as they had expected, rather they were both frantically firing arrows at an as yet unknown terror. As they came closer, they strained their eyes to try to view the creature that Aerlyn and Lexon were struggling against.

The creature came into sight, quickly advancing on the two heroes. Their weapons appeared to be having little or no effect against the huge, green amoeba like creature. Its bulky body pulsated with bursting pustules of slime as it slithered closer and closer to Aerlyn and Lexon; an unblinking, single red eye stared at its prey and whipping tendrils thrashed back and forth trying to grasp at the elves.

The team gazed at the monstrous creature as they frantically paddled to help Aerlyn and Lexon. Their attention was so consumed by the activities at the edge of the sewer that none of them noticed a stealthy, humanoid figure scaling the vessel from the dark, murky depths of the sewer waters.

The boat drew close to the battling heroes and the team prepared to disembark, weapons at the ready to destroy this odious creature.

"Don't let it touch you!" yelled Aerlyn to the crew as she hastily restrung another arrow to fire at the advancing creature.

"Why?" questioned a tall human as he readied himself to launch his mighty spear.

Before Aerlyn had time to answer, the bulk of the amoeba had diverted its attention to the commotion from the boat and lashed out two long tentacles. With deadly accuracy, the tentacles wrapped themselves tightly around the waist of the tall human that had called to Aerlyn. At the same time, the second tentacle caught around the waist of another victim. A cry of anguish came from the ravaged face of the Piranhaman who had climbed aboard the boat hoping to feast on the crew but who had in fact now become the prey.

The two captives were hurled around by the ravenous tentacles like rag dolls. A sickening snap echoed around the tunnels as, first, the spine of the human and, then, the spine of the Piranhaman were snapped. Limp and lifeless, the two bodies were whipped back towards the pulsating body of the menacing amoeba creature. The tentacles dropped the bodies into the throbbing, gash like mouth that formed the centre of the beast and they were instantly absorbed, deep into the digestive system of the monster.

Dodging the flailing tentacles, the remaining warriors looked on in horror. The tentacles were grasping at anything. One gripped hard to the raised axe of a dwarf and it was ripped from his strong hands and thrust into the digestive system of the amoeba just as the two bodies had been.

Raging at the beast, the dwarf bellowed, "You great pile of manure, that axe was given to me by my grandfather! I will reclaim it!" He spat the words venomously and his anger burned passionately in his eyes. The dwarf grasped two more axes from his waistband and leapt towards one of the tentacles. Fearlessly, he hacked at the whipping tendril. The tendril moved at lightening speed and the dwarf's initial attack only resulted in a hail of sparks as the mighty blades of the axes crashed against stone, with thunderous clangs. The dwarf persisted and, on his second attack, struck lucky and pinned a throbbing tendril with one axe and sliced through its writhing length with his second axe. The released stump squirmed and gushed copious amounts of green stained fluid like a high pressure water hose. Out with the fluid poured the flesh stripped bones of the digested human and Piranhaman, closely followed by the dwarf's axe, still complete.

The other heroes and warriors, desperate to kill the beast, had watched the actions of the brave dwarf and, having witnessed the flow of bones and the axe, were invigorated in their attempts to destroy this deadly beast. Mustering all their strength, they each attacked the tentacles. As each tentacle was sliced, more and more of the green tinged slime poured onto the sewer floor and ran into the sewer water. As more fluid ran out of the beast, it started to diminish in size and the remaining tentacles slowed in their attacks as the life force of the beast ebbed away. With one last flailing whip, the last tentacle was sliced by Lexon and the final remnants of fluid drained away. The beast was dead and the warriors were safe.

The weary comrades dropped their weapons and sank to the ground, exhausted, every muscle in their bodies crying out in pain. But, they were alive and would live to fight another day. Unfortunately that day would be sooner than any of them had imagined.

. Chapter Twenty .

THE BATTLECRY

IT WAS now twilight and the sewer tunnels were frantic. Reports had come in from the scouts dispersed throughout the region that Numbar had gathered together his army much earlier than the resistance had expected and they now hurriedly assembled equipment and readied themselves for battle.

Once preparations were complete, every single orc, human, demon, elf or dwarf trained by the heroes, emerged from the sewers and started to make their way through the slums towards the Imperial tower of Numbar's castle; here they would wait for daybreak. Each knew that they were to partake in the most momentous battle of their lives. A battle that had raged across the many ages of man and elf and was now to take place again here and now. Good versus evil.

As the first rays of light broke through the pitch black of the night sky the rebel soldiers were ready.

High in the safety of the tallest tower, Numbar looked down over his vast army of ragtag recruits brought from all over the city of Krakara and beyond. Robbers, muggers and murderers had been forced to join the army. Deviants, gang members and pirates had joined readily, enticed by the promise of valuable rewards. Young humans also stood alongside these vagabonds, desperate to revel in the glory of battle and to be worshipped as war heroes. Many more had been blackmailed and tortured into joining the ranks of Numbar's corrupt army.

Using mystical, demonic forces and pledging his allegiance to the dark, evil Lord Ladracsin, Numbar had summoned devils from the pits of hell in exchange for the innocent souls of children, which were to be tortured through all time. Never had so much pure evil accumulated in one place. As Numbar gazed down, his dark eyes flashed and a menacing smile turned the corners of his thin lips. Soon his empire would reach further than he had ever imagined. He would be all powerful.

Meanwhile, unknown to Numbar, the resistance gathered themselves and prepared to make siege on the Imperial tower. As its warriors steadied their nerves, the hero leaders rallied their spirits with rousing and heartfelt speeches.

"Friends, fellow clerics and champions! Today is a day of reckoning! In my dreams, I have foreseen this day! I have seen how we will overcome the torment of battle, how we will cheat death and destruction and how we shall retake this Holy land!"

"Epelorn foretold this to me in a vision. Many of us will soon come to dwell in the great, vast realms of Epelorn, I promise you! You will meet with him as you fight for all that is good and for God!" Harthor thundered.

As he finished his rousing speech, he held high his sword and the clouds in the sky parted above them. The rebel warriors all followed suit and thrust their weapons high into the air, roaring a deafening battle cry.

. Chapter Twenty One .

LET BATTLE COMMENCE

STARTLED, Numbar gazed down from his Imperial tower; he had not expected opposition so close to his own headquarters. He had heard rumours of rebel soldiers lurking in the sewers below the dark city but had reasoned that his zombie horde would have reduced them to nothing more than a few broken remnants.

The rebel army before him looked more organized and committed than he had anticipated. Still, no matter, he sighed to himself complacently, no match for my mighty Rolxmarr.

With that thought, he turned and addressed the mighty horde he had assembled within the Imperial Tower, "Scum of the earth! I will forever torment you if you do not do my bidding and defeat whatever force opposes us."

The rabble below booed and jeered at their leader's words. Numbar raised his gnarled hand and crushed a herbal root that he had lifted from his bejeweled tunic. Instantly, a blue vapour spiraled from his bony fingertips and snaked its evil path like a venomous serpent down to each and every member of Numbar's evil army.

Each inhaled the corrosive vapour and fell to the ground in agony as the sinister magic instigated the elemental changes that would cause the demonic transformation on a massive scale. The entire army began to morph into vile and deadly Rolxmarr.

Outside the main wall, the rebel army began to move forward. Harthor roared the advance, "Now is our chance! To glory!" It was as if he knew that any delay would lead to annihilation and, as he cried, every warrior plunged forward in desperation, swords drawn, axes raised and bows loaded.

"Leave no survivors!" Numbar grinned haughtily as he commanded his formidable army. The transformed Rolxmarr horde scrambled forward with a blood curdling war cry. Frothing at the mouth, they craved the blood that ran through their enemy and they made their attack. The great gates opened and the Rolxmarr spilled forth.

The elves had taken the lead in the charge towards the now opening gates that had blocked their path to Numbar. Aided by their light footed agility, they sped across the undulating terrain, firing a lethal hail of arrows into the horde that poured through the gates.

Struggling with the weight of their armour and the shortness of their legs, the dwarves advanced at a much slower pace, panting for breath and stumbling in the straggling grasses. Their axes were, however, held high and they were ready to do battle.

Running swiftly, Lexon and Aerlyn cast their bows over their shoulders and drew their trusted weapons. Lexon pulled his long sword that had been safely stowed at his hip and Aerlyn withdrew a pair of curved daggers from their leather holsters. Close behind, Harthor had his razor sharp broad sword raised valiantly and it glinted brilliantly in the sunlight. It shone brightly like a beacon of hope in the darkness and all who saw it were inspired as Harthor's courage spread throughout the ranks of the rebellion.

Zuboko crossed his long sword and his ancient staff together like scorpion pincers. Mollynia was close to his side and was armed with an orb. The orb glowed with an intense blue light which pulsated with every advancing step that Mollynia took towards her enemy. She glanced over at Zuboko, who returned her strong gaze and he smiled even in the frenzy of the attack. Mollynia could see the other rebel leaders to the left of Zuboko; Gronkyear and Cruntck, weapons aloft and their lips moving but no sound escaping, as they silently mouthed their sacred rituals to their Gods.

As the two armies drew nearer to one another, Mollynia pulled back her arm and, without breaking stride, hurled the glowing orb directly at the advancing horde. The intensity of the orb increased as it came closer to the Rolxmarr beasts. As it hit the ground at the front of their ranks, an inferno of dazzling bright light and heat ruptured through the deadly beasts, depleting their numbers on impact. Simultaneously, a hail of arrows made their mark and more Rolxmarr fell to the ground. The swarming creatures did not break stride and advanced towards the rebellion stepping on the remains of their fellow warriors.

Zuboko called to Mollynia, "Good strike, only about a billion to go!"

Mollynia smiled back.

With a thunderous roar, the two armies came together!

. Chapter Twenty Two .

THE FALL OF THE IMPERIAL TOWER

THE entire elf line was decimated in a matter of seconds. Limbs were ripped from torsos and cast aside. In desperation, a gallant elf lunged forwards, throwing himself onto the back of a Rolxmarr beast. The forward momentum of the Rolxmarr was too much for the fragile bones of the elf and he was crushed instantly. His lifeless body dropped to the ground and was trampled by another horrendous beast.

Lexon and Aerlyn stayed as close together as possible, trying to watch out for each other in the madness of the battle. Aerlyn had leapt onto the back of a beast and plunged her daggers in rapid succession deep into the creature's back and neck. Writhing, the beast tried to unseat Aerlyn but its efforts were useless and with one final moan, it dropped to the ground, its soul falling even deeper into the abyss of hell.

Lexon had artfully dissected the threatening, pummeling arms of a Rolxmarr and was mercilessly driving his blade into the depths of the creature's chest. Close by, Cruntck had adopted the same tactic as Lexon; disabling the beasts by removing their deadly appendages. Cruntck was then, however, using their detached arms as weapons and piercing their abdomens with the razor sharp scales. Death was instantaneous.

Harthor was in the thick of the battle, leading the strong humans bravely. They had avenged the slaughtered elves but were now starting to be slain as they themselves were getting more and more outnumbered; relentlessly, reserves of Rolxmarr swarmed through the castle gates.

Harthor butchered two Rolxmarr at the same time, as his trusty blade cut through one and then another. Deftly, he withdrew the blade from depths of one beast's body and a gush of blood spurted, splattering his already blood stained tunic and armour. Twisting the sharp point backwards, it penetrated another creature. A further twist and the beast had all of its vital organs severed. With flailing arms, it crashed to the ground, which was now carpeted by a thick layer of bodies both good and evil.

The Rolxmarr were punishing the rebellion. Demons and dark elves fought nobly but were no match for the depraved Rolxmarr which hacked and slashed in a frenzy of death and destruction.

Gronkyear and Mollynia were surrounded by advancing Rolxmarr. Their comrades lay motionless all about them in a carpet of blood and death. The two backed away slowly until they were forced to stop by an embankment. Twisting his sword at the salivating beasts and with adrenaline coursing through his veins, Gronkyear called out, "Come on then, you foul beasts! Who wants a piece of me?"

Still the creatures advanced. Gronkyear cut and thrust with his blade. Blood splashed and sprayed in every direction, but still the enemy came forth. Every thrust of his blade weakened Gronkyear. The attacks from the Rolxmarr were relentless. He was becoming so battle weary that he could barely swing his blade. The Rolxmarr moved closer. Gronkyear stood tall, knowing that his end was near.

Just as Gronkyear thought he had drawn his final breath, Mollynia pulled out a sparkling green gem and, chanting an incantation, pointed its blazing green reflection at the Rolxmarr thronged around them. The Rolxmarr were suddenly immobile, frozen to the spot. Re-energised, Gronkyear lifted his sword and, with one mighty slice, shattered the frozen beasts into thousands of tiny pieces like shards of glass. Impressed, Gronkyear shouted his thanks to Mollynia who was already deep in battle with another deadly adversary.

Zuboko was amongst the foray with the dwarves, who were battling heartily and with a passion that Zuboko had not thought possible; they were, however, struggling to make any impact on their foe. Dismayed, Zuboko witnessed the two dwarves, who yesterday had massacred the terrifying amoeba creature, being barbarically eviscerated by two frenzied Rolxmarr. Their mutilated bodies, now beyond recognition, fell to the ground and lay buried beneath their unfortunate comrades.

Harthor sensed the battle was nearly over. The rebellion would be overcome. The power of Numbar's created army had been so immense. Victory would be to the dark and evil side. As Harthor decapitated one Rolxmarr and parried another, his eyes fell over the devastation of the battlefield. Good lay with evil in a sea of blood and guts. Harthor parried the frenzy of razor scales that lumbered towards him. The beast suddenly fell forwards to its doom, a hail of arrows piercing deep into its spiny back. Looking up, Harthor saw Aerlyn hand on quiver, reloading.

Standing on a small hillock, Zuboko twirled his ancient staff like a baton. Each time the staff made contact with a lethal beast, flashes of electricity emanated from within and electrocuted the evil creatures. Mounds of charred flesh surrounded the hillock and the rank smell of burnt flesh drifted across the battlefield on the breeze. Leaping across the scorched masses, Zuboko made his way slowly, arduously, to his comrade Cruntck, twisting and twirling the staff in the direction of every oncoming beast.

Cruntck was fighting valiantly and was trying to remove his battleaxe from the skull of a monster before his next enemy made its attack. He struggled briefly to remove the axe, but in vain; not only had the axe severed the skull it had embedded itself deep in the rock underneath. There was no time to struggle to release it. Hastily Cruntck grabbed a highly decorated and surprisingly light elf blade from the massacred corpse of a Rolxmarr. He spun the blood smeared blade elegantly and sliced it across the throat of the Rolxmarr that rose upon him. The head dropped backwards, suspended by only a few slithers of flesh. The beast crashed to its death.

Astonishingly, the small group of surviving rebel warriors was starting to inch its way forward towards the tower.

Then suddenly and without warning, a monstrous, black fireball screeched through the air and crashed full force into Gronkyear, sending him sprawling backwards. He was immediately engulfed by black flames and Cruntck, too far away to help his close friend, looked on in anguish as Gronkyear desperately tried to extinguish his burning flesh to no avail.

Gronkyear, like all Comoq demons, was possessed of slimy sebaceous skin and, as a result, burned much slower than human flesh. The long, excruciating death that Gronkyear was experiencing was brought to a sudden climax by a looming Rolxmarr that tore Gronkyear from limb to limb. Gronkyear's smoldering remains lay scattered across the battlefield, his soul soaring high to the heavens, released from earthly pain. The first of the rebel leaders had fallen.

For a second, Cruntck hung his head at the memory of his friend and his heart filled with sorrow at his passing. Aerlyn looked up to the tower where the black fireball had originated from. There, she saw Numbar staring down at them, his face filled with glee at the destruction being wreaked by his army. With a reverberating flurry, a single arrow left Aerlyn's bow. It soared towards the tower, high in the air, towards Numbar. The mark was accurate and the arrow sped at Numbar, homing in, right between his loathsome eyes. Seconds before impact, the arrow suddenly stopped, hovered for a second more and then disintegrated into ashes that were blown on the breeze back down from the height of the tower to the bloodied earth. Numbar laughed spitefully down at the heroes as the battle raged on.

The death of Gronkyear spurred on the remaining six heroes and they rallied, silently renewing their vow to rid the world of the evil tyrant, Numbar.

They inched forward again; they had somehow managed to battle their way to the entrance gates of the tower through which the army of Rolxmarr had emerged not so long ago. Numbar, as arrogant as ever, had not contemplated the possibility that the rebellion would have survived this long and the gateway was neither barricaded nor guarded. Aerlyn, the first to reach the gates, darted through, closely followed by Zuboko and Lexon. Mollynia, as ever, was not far from Zuboko. Only Harthor and Cruntck of the hero leaders remained in battle, supported by a small group of humans and dwarves, continuing to resist fiercely.

"Harthor! Flee! I'll hold them off! Go kill that warlock! Here take my axe, you need it more than me!" Cruntck roared deafeningly.

"May the gods bless you!" Harthor prayed as he grasped the sacred axe from Cruntck and clutched it in his huge, sweaty hand. Harthor launched himself into the interior of the Tower, rolling and just avoiding the strike of an awaiting Rolxmarr.

Behind him, Harthor could hear the valiant war cries of his fellow hero, Cruntck and the remaining rebel soldiers. Their cries rang out strong but soon silence descended as they were finally overcome by the marauding attacks of the Rolxmarr. Cruntck had forsaken this world and passed to the other side; his bravery would always be remembered.

Just behind him, Harthor turned quickly to see a mass of thrusting, razor scaled arms. Then, from the centre of the melee, arose a single hero.

Cruntck sprang from the pile, slicing mortal blows with the elvish blade. Battered and bleeding profusely, he was not finished yet. He stood before the tower door halting every attempt by a Rolxmarr demon to pass him. Mustering all his might he thrust the blade at the advancing horde and roared to Harthor, "Hurry, you fool! I can't last much longer!"

Harthor hurried on and quickly caught up with the remaining heroes. Having entered the inner sanctum of the tower, they were trying to locate the stairway that would lead them to the evil leader and provide them with the chance to end this battle. The room was dark with no natural lighting and seemed eerily quiet after the intense noise of the battle outside the tower's walls.

The heroes stayed close to the walls which were icy cold to the touch and silky smooth. A single flaming torch cast a shadowy light from high on the wall. As their eyes became accustomed to the dimly lit room, they could make out the shape of two doors. Which to choose?

"Hurry! I'll go through this one and you all go through that one!" suggested Harthor persuasively.

"Fine!" Zuboko panted, exhausted from the battle.

Meanwhile, Cruntck was still holding firm against the Rolxmarr horde; determined to delay the retaking of the tower, he felt the reassuring snap of another enemy's neck as his strong hands twisted with all their might. By now, he was standing on a small plateau of dead bodies which had gathered by the tower door against which his back was firmly pressed; he had fought proudly but was nearing complete exhaustion when he felt his body flinch in pain; he was hit!

Harthor took the first door. He opened it silently and entered the room within. Stepping forwards, his breath caught in his throat at what lay before him. Across the room by the far wall stood a huge, ruby and gold statue. Harthor recognised it immediately. The statue was a shrine to Ladracsin. From the statue's grotesque mouth flowed an endless stream of blood drizzling downwards. Surrounding the statue were more statues, highly decorated and brandishing deadly weapons.

Chained to the wall were the remains of sacrifices in the name of Ladracsin. The rotting corpses of what looked like elves. In front of the statue was an ornate table, laden with jars of ingredients for dark magic. The strong aroma of incense stifled the air in the room. Harthor could sense pure evil in this room but there were no stairs to be seen.

Just as Harthor entered this doorway, the others had passed through theirs. The four heroes made their way stealthily past row upon row of cages. Most were empty but some were still occupied. All manner of evil fiend could be found in the cages; all waiting to be used for Numbar's evil purposes; hellhounds and vampires, Ankh worms, giant venomous spiders and trolls. All lay in a deep, unnatural sleep, no doubt drugged by Numbar and they barely stirred at the presence of the four heroes. As they crept by, they spotted a stairway at the far side of the cages.

Outside, Cruntck's noble resistance was nearing an end; he had been hit by an iridescent, purple strobe beam directed from the height of the tower by Numbar. Cruntck gazed down at his hands as they became swollen and wrinkled as he stood on the plateau of bodies. He was ageing; the beam was draining the life force from him by the second. He felt his spine hunch over as his skeleton became disfigured, his joints grew gnarled and his skin tissue paper thin. His hair turned white and his eyesight started to fail him. Suddenly, a strong wind whipped around the tower walls and in its wake left nothing but dust where, moments before, had stood the mighty heroic figure of Cruntck. High in the safety of his tower, Numbar laughed down, reveling in the demise of his latest foe.

Harthor turned to leave the room in order to follow his companions into the other doorway. As he made his way back, he heard a strange scraping sound and rumbling. It was metal on stone. Warily Harthor glanced over his shoulder, just in time to see the statues moving from their mantles and stepping to the ground. The statues began to march towards Harthor drawing their scimitars. Harthor backed away. He brushed against a blood red curtain that draped the wall and was grabbed from behind by the neck. To Harthor's shock, he had been grabbed by the curtain which had now started to tighten around his neck and chest, stopping the flow of oxygen. Harthor's face started to turn red and then purple as he frantically tried to release a knife from his belt. As the curtains tightened their grip, the army of statues made their way closer and closer. Desperate for air, Harthor thrashed his arms wildly, trying to locate a weapon. In relief, his fingers closed on the sheath that held his dagger. With a swift upward thrust, Harthor slashed at the curtain until it no longer had a grip around his neck; he readily sucked in the oxygen to his starved lungs.

The curtains had slowed Harthor's escape and the statues were already upon him. He smashed Cruntck's axe against the head of one of the statues with such force that it caused the statue to wobble precariously and, after a few teetering seconds, it crashed full weight to the marble floor and smashed. The sound echoed around the room just as the wooden door was battered down sending splinters of wood flying into the room. In streamed Rolxmarr, eager to seek out the remaining rebel warriors.

As soon as the Rolxmarr entered the room, their attention was immediately distracted away from Harthor by the statues that glimmered and glistened in the flickering torch light.

"Oooh, shiny!" the Rolxmarr growled in unison. Ignoring Harthor, the Rolxmarr grabbed at the shining gold jewellery which adorned the statues, hypnotised by its brilliance and beauty.

The statues deflected the lunges of the Rolxmarr and began to fight back. As the statues and the Rolxmarr set about one another, Harthor saw his chance to escape and swiftly made his way to the other doorway to catch up with his fellow heroes.

Meanwhile, Aerlyn and the others had started to sprint towards the stairway; they had heard the unmistakable sounds of cage bolts unlocking and releasing behind them. All efforts to stay quiet were forgotten as they realised they would soon be joined by the occupants of the cages.

Almost at once, all the cage doors swung open, awakening the sleeping beasts within. Within moments, every snarling creature was in pursuit, hungry for fresh meat. The creatures attacked with speed and ferocity. Lexon swung his sword just in time as two hell hounds soared through the air from the top of a cage. Two severed bodies plummeted to the ground, writhing in agony as the last signs of life ebbed away. Mollynia was grabbed by a ravenous vampire. He thrust back her dark neck exposing the pulsating vein. Mollynia struggled in vain as the vampire prepared to plunge its brutal fangs into her flesh and drink her pure blood. Just as Mollynia prepared for the pain of her death, the vampire relaxed its grip and fell forwards, trapping her beneath him; she was, however, only trapped for a moment as the vampire almost immediately evaporated into dust. Aerlyn had pierced the demon's black heart with a wooden arrow and slain the unholy menace.

Zuboko was defending himself against an extraordinarily gigantic troll. For every step the troll advanced towards Zuboko, it received a blast of white hot flame directly in the face. Aerlyn now joined forces with Zuboko and began to shower the troll with as many arrows as she could release at one time. It finally collapsed to the floor with a resounding thud and crushed many cages with its enormous bulk.

Aerlyn, closely followed by Mollynia, had reached the bottom of the staircase; as the battle raged behind them, they slowly ascending the twisting steps. Any element of surprise was bound to have been lost with the chaos of this last battle. They approached the doorway at the top. However, it was not Numbar who was surprised when they reached the room at the top of the tower, it was the heroes. For there, waiting patiently was Numbar.

. Chapter Twenty Three .

CHAOS AWAKES

"Ahh, you must be . . . Aerlyn. I have heard about you from Lord Ladracsin. He tells me that you and your half breed brother, Lexon, fled like cowards from the pitiable City of so-called Saints at the slightest hint of conflict. He also told me that your father died squealing like a baby and begging for mercy when Lord Ladracsin's emissary slit his throat!" Numbar sneered menacingly in Aerlyn's head as he communicated with her telepathically.

"No, NO he didn't! My father died a glorious and honourable death, in battle!" Aerlyn rasped back, her mind racing.

"Ah now, I see you start to doubt the truth of that story, my dear! Deep down, you know that you belong to a race of cowardly half breeds, more likely to flee and hide than to display courage! " whispered Numbar, an ominous tone in his voice.

"No! No, he didn't" Aerlyn screamed violently at Numbar. This time, she spoke out loud.

Mollynia, surprised at this sudden outburst, turned to Aerlyn, "What didn't he do?" she asked, unaware of the telepathic exchange between Numbar and Aerlyn.

"But he did, my sweet, and Lord Ladracsin had him and his miserable offspring put to a slow and lingering death! One by one, he killed them all!" Numbar spoke with the chill of a ruthless killer.

"Aerlyn, what didn't he do?" Mollynia asked again, this time moving closer to Aerlyn, unsure what was happening or what was going to happen next. Mollynia stopped in her tracks. Numbar had cast a forcefield which held the two heroes confined.

"In fact, my dear, I see no need for your dark elf companion and I do wish to try out something new that I have been working on!" Without hesitation and before Aerlyn had realised what Numbar was saying, he had thrown a silver ball of light towards Mollynia. The silver ball engulfed Mollynia. She fought and thrashed, but her resistance was futile and within seconds, Mollynia had become a solid silver statue.

Aerlyn looked on helpless as her companion was transformed. Suddenly, she felt overwhelmed by a deep sense of sadness passing through her. Already today, she had seen many brave souls destroyed in the fight for good over evil. In the last few days, she had lost loyal comrades and friends and now she had now been told that her family had been cruelly butchered by the evil master of the creature which sat before her.

As deep sorrow flooded Aerlyn's heart, changes began to course through her body.

Lifting her head, her eyes flashed bright yellow. On either hand, dark symbols burned into her flesh. Chaos was rising from within.

Huge claws protruded from her fingertips like sharp talons. Where previously had been the delicate, graceful features of an elf was now the hideous visage of a chaos demon; leathery, scarred flesh, vicious fangs and a face contorted with a burning desire to destroy.

"Is that supposed to scare me?" Numbar sneered wickedly as he cast another silver ball of light, this time towards Aerlyn.

Aerlyn glided through the air and somersaulted over the silver ball as it crashed into where she had been standing. Then as fast as lightning, she bounded towards Numbar.

Her wild, chaotic side had been locked deep within the elf's body for nearly six thousand years and was incredibly hungry.

She loomed over Numbar and raised her talloned hand, poised to lash out at his face. Suddenly, the chaotic Aerlyn was cast aside like a puppet. It was as though an invisible, sinister hand had grabbed her and was dragging her across the marble floor towards the balcony. Her claws scratched and scraped at the marble floor but she could get no purchase. Seconds later, she was hanging onto the side of the balcony, her weight pulling her down. Again, she felt the invisible force and it launched her from the balcony down into the midst of the Rolxmarr horde below.

"I don't think we'll be seeing her again!" Numbar laughed harshly.

"Now, what to do with you?" he pondered, staring at the statue of Mollynia. "Hmm, I think I prefer gold to silver!" Numbar sneered. He waved his gnarled hand towards the statue and instantly it changed from gleaming silver to a brilliant gold. "Unfortunately, I do not like the subject of the statue!" a wicked glint in his eye. Arrogantly, he moved his finger in the direction of the statue and it became a golden statue of himself. Numbar spoke angrily at the statue, "You! What is your name?"

A grating sound emanated from the statue and its lips began to move, "I have no name, my master, as you have not given me one."

"Good, good! Now tell me! What of Mollynia?" he commanded.

"She is dead, my Lord!" whispered the statue almost inaudibly.

. Chapter Twenty Four .

THE FURY OF AERLYN

THE entire collection of Numbar's caged 'pets' now lay dead at the feet of Harthor, Lexon and Zuboko.

The three were unscathed, but battle weary and ready for the whole episode to be over. There was no time to rest; they must catch up with Aerlyn and Mollynia. Who knew what evil lay at the top of the tower. Some time had passed since the two had ascended the stairway. Besides, they felt it would not be long before more Rolxmarr would be joining them. Zuboko lead the way up the stairway. He had taken only a couple of steps when the Rolxmarr burst into the room.

"Zuboko, go and kill Numbar! We shall hold them off!" commanded Harthor bruskly. Zuboko didn't hesitate and continued upward as Lexon and Harthor turned and braced themselves for more bloodshed.

Beyond the entrance to the room, the Rolxmarr were in dire trouble. Their once mighty army which had crushed the rebellion was being torn apart by a single enemy.

The chaotic Aerlyn was ravaging their numbers. Her huge talons sliced at their flesh and, with her insatiable appetite, she gorged on their blood. The Rolxmarr were proving no challenge for the frenzied creature and, one by one, they fell to the fury of her raging attacks. Claws drawn to full length, she ripped through victim after victim, pausing only to lick her bloodied talons before attacking, again and again.

. Chapter Twenty Five .

THE DRUID'S FURY

ZUBOKO barged into Numbar's room at the top of the tower, staff ready to do battle with the sorcerer.

"Ahh, Zuboko! Finally, two great minds meet! I do not wish to kill you. Yet! Firstly, I would like to make you a proposition. My master would like you to change allegiance and join our order. The order that gave you your markings at birth. Your kin!" offered Numbar.

"So in other words you want me to become a slave of Ladracsin!" Zuboko spat back.

"Hmm, that is disappointing. Lord Ladracsin will not be pleased that you have rejected his offer. Now, I will have to kill you!" continued Numbar, cackling as he rose from his golden throne.

As he rose, he thrust out his hand and from the corner of the room a red staff first moved and then sped effortlessly to its master's outstretched palm. A chill ran down Zuboko's spine. The hairs at the back of his neck stood on end. The red staff was the ultimate symbol of darkness and of the ultimate evil, Ladracsin.

Numbar swiftly grasped the staff and attacked Zuboko. A terrifying bolt burst from its tip, aiming directly at Zuboko. Zuboko's reactions were quick and he easily blocked the strike, creating a forcefield around himself, deflecting the bolt and causing it to crash into a nearby statue which was immediately incinerated. This time it was Zuboko who retaliated, summoning an intense force within his staff and unleashing it with all the power he could muster at Numbar. The thunderbolt hurtled across the room. Numbar countered the attack with a blast of pure evil. The two forces collided in the centre of the room. The impact was deafening as the two massive streams of energy exploded.

The druid and the warlock were quick to protect themselves from the force but the room, in which they fought, felt the full impact of the explosion. Debris lay everywhere. Fire spread to anything that was flammable. Soon, the room filled with acrid, black smoke. The two battled on, each attacking the other with stronger and stronger magic.

At the bottom of the stairs, Harthor and Lexon were knocked to the ground as the earth shuddered at the explosion caused by the battling wizards.

"Sounds like Zuboko is having fun!" called Harthor to Lexon as they struggled to get to their feet. Lexon grimaced in reply.

He was growing weary, but was it his imagination or were the two heroes actually starting to drive the Rolxmarr back? No, it wasn't his imagination; the Rolxmarr were definitely losing momentum. With this realization, Lexon battled on, a surge of hope filled his heart and a burst of adrenalin pulsed through his veins.

Harthor's sword slashed through the last of the Rolxmarr within the caged room. They had cleared the room. For the first time that day, they felt they were starting to prevail.

Moving towards the exit, they could hear screams of terror from the Rolxmarr outside. Some unknown force was devastating their numbers. If the force was attacking the Rolxmarr, then surely it was a good thing. The force must be in alliance with them against the evil of Numbar.

As the two neared the exit, a cloaked figure ran into the room. The cloak was in tatters and stained with blood and mud. Even in its ragged condition, Lexon recognised the cloak as his sister's.

The tiny figure stopped in front of the two heroes, shoulders heaving up and down as the figure panted for breath. Slowly the figure lifted its head. The delicate features of Aerlyn's beautiful face were distorted by deep cuts and beads of sweat trickled down her forehead.

Looking up at her two comrades with wide, clear eyes she spoke in short gasps, "Hey, I . . . just . . . killed the … horde!"

All signs of her chaotic side had evaporated. Lexon ran forwards and threw his arms around his sister, squeezing her until she coughed for breath and begged him to stop.

Another explosion reverberated through the tower and the three raced up the stairway to help Zuboko.

Cautiously, they looked into the room, or what was left of the room. The smoke slowly cleared and was replaced by a web of static electricity which fizzed and sizzled around the room, releasing fountains of sparks.

Numbar turned his cold gaze away from Zuboko and looked at the three heroes. Instantly, the three were catapulted at the opposite wall. Their bodies were suspended by an invisible force as chains swiftly curled around their wrists and ankles. Their struggles were futile as they were shackled helplessly to the wall, looking down at the warlock and the druid.

Turning back towards Zuboko, Numbar spoke, his voice icy and full of menace.

"Well Zuboko, shall we make a deal? Join the order of my master and your friends will live. Do not join and they will die. They will die an awful death and you will watch!"

"Don't do it!" called Harthor. The chains tightened around him. As they tightened, another chain swirled across the wall like a deadly snake hunting its prey and coiled around Harthor's throat, making him gasp for air.

"Shut up or you will die now!" ordered Numbar, seething at the interruption. Numbar was starting to lose his patience. He was desperate to do his master's bidding.

Zuboko saw that Numbar was distracted and took his chance, raining blow after blow at Numbar.

Distracted, Numbar was for once, too slow to react and the first bolt hit him full blast on the head. He recoiled, the pain blinding him. With no time to recover and defend himself, another and another bolt made direct contact with Numbar's skull.

Falling backwards, Numbar grasped his head with both hands. The pain was excruciating. As he screamed in agony, his staff fell to the ground. Still blasting relentlessly at his enemy, Zuboko stepped forwards and seized the red staff. Hastily he thrust his hand inside his tunic to grasp the artefact that Harthor, Gronkyear and Cruntck had retrieved. Gazing down at his palm, Zuboko briefly admired the glistening gemstone before driving it securely into the upper most point of Numbar's red staff. The merging of the two relics created a mighty weapon; one which Zuboko could use to destroy Numbar.

Zuboko held the staff and pointed it at Numbar, who was still writhing in agony from the direct head blows. Numbar did not know what had hit him; the force of the blast was so devastating. A pulsating beam radiated directly at Numbar.

Numbar was motionless on the ground. Blood seeped from his eye sockets, ears and nose. Numbar was dead!

Taking the staff in two hands, Zuboko cracked it hard across his leg. The staff broke in two like a stick. From the broken edges poured a shiny grey liquid which pooled on the floor momentarily and then disappeared. An overwhelming relief spread through the whole of Zuboko's body. He had finally defeated Numbar. The exhausted wizard sank to his knees.

Remembering his fellow heroes still suspended by their chains, Zuboko turned to release them from their shackles. As he did so, his face contorted with agony as his body was squeezed by an incredible force. What was this? Zuboko was confused. Numbar was dead. This evil should have stopped.

The force continued to squeeze the life from Zuboko so he could barely breathe. He felt his body being lifted and he was spun around to where Numbar had been lying on the ground.

To his horror, Numbar was standing once again.

"Do not think I am so easy to destroy, you fool of a druid!" Numbar laughed hideously.

Zuboko continued to gaze at the vile creature that stood before him but he was conscious that something was happening behind Numbar. Following Zuboko's gaze, Numbar turned to see one of his statues moving from its base, weapon raised and slowly, stiffly walking towards Zuboko.

Arrogantly, Numbar raised his hands and exclaimed, "Ahh, do you see Zuboko, even my servants want to destroy you!"

The statue continued around towards Zuboko. Zuboko had no staff to defend himself. He had put it down in order to smash the red staff. What a fool he had been.

Seeing the sadness and desperation in Zuboko's eyes, Numbar continued smugly, "Oh, and Zuboko, I do believe you have met my servant before but you may not have recognised her. May I introduce you to Mollynia!"

The resigned sadness in Zuboko's eyes was instantly replaced by a look of horror as he realised the evil that had transformed his Mollynia, and a solitary, "No!" escaped from his lips.

The golden statue drew its sword. Zuboko gazed at the golden face. It was the face of his enemy, but looking deep into the statue's eyes, he was sure he could see the soul of Mollynia. A single tear fell from its eye and trickled down its smooth, golden skin.

As the tear splashed to the floor, the statue twisted violently round and catapulted the sword at Numbar; time seemed to stand still as it arced across the room, rotating soundlessly as it sliced through Numbar's neck decapitating him instantly. His head tumbled to the floor, a shocked look of disbelief frozen for ever on his deathly features.

Zuboko threw himself bodily at the golden statue. Calling out her name, Zuboko held the statue close, but it no longer moved and the eyes that had exposed Mollynia's soul were now closed. She was gone. As Numbar's evil had died all his evil doings had ceased too.

"Farewell Mollynia!" sighed Zuboko.

. Chapter Twenty Six .

THE QUEST CONTINUES

A DULL echo resonated through the desolate, destroyed streets as Zuboko made his way through the bloodied pathways. A low, metallic clanging rang out bleakly as the last of the memorial stones was hammered into place. It was hard to believe that a week before this place had been a busy, bustling market, full of street sellers and tradesmen. Now, it was a different picture; the evil beasts that had fallen in the battle were now piled in rotting heaps. Zuboko looked up to see Harthor burying the last of the rebel soldier remains. "Ashes to ashes, dust to dust," whispered Harthor, head bowed in respect as he completed the burial chant.

Zuboko's heart was filled with sorrow for his rebellion comrades; they had fought so valiantly but had died so brutally, however his thoughts always returned to Mollynia.

Filled with grief, Zuboko had used his magic to create a statue of Mollynia just as he remembered her; a glistening smile on her lips and the tear on her cheek.

At the foot of the statue Zuboko dropped to his knees; immediately, the surrounding ground was carpeted with delicate bluebells. Their fragrance, strong and sweet, overpowering the odour of death and destruction.

Aerlyn and Lexon were high in the Imperial Tower, salvaging whatever they could that was not evil. Lexon stuffed his sack with an array of potions that he thought would be of use in their continued battle against Ladracsin and then turned to take them downstairs. Lexon had not noticed Numbar's carcass, which remained where it had fallen at the end of the battle and suddenly tripped. Lexon hurtled forwards, losing his balance and reaching for the wall to save himself. The sack smashed to the floor. Aerlyn, startled by the sudden crash, jumped nimbly to her feet and turned to see the multicoloured liquids seeping from the sack, hissing and steaming as the concoctions mixed. Lexon jumped back as the potions trickled towards him and muttered to himself for being so clumsy. In his dismay at losing the potions, Lexon kicked out at Numbar's decapitated head and sent it spinning across the room and down the stairs.

"Don't stand in any of the spillage" instructed Aerlyn as she nimbly hopped over the puddles of potion. "You could end up with no legs and a tail!"

Lexon looked at his sister with an ironic smile and then followed Aerlyn down the stairs to meet with Harthor and Zuboko as arranged.

The heroes had arranged to meet and pay their last respects to the formidable pair, Cruntck and Gronkyear. Standing together, the memorials to the warriors were a fitting tribute to their bravery and courage. A huge marble urn held the ashes of Gronkyear, whose mortal body had been ripped apart; the heroes had therefore cremated him with the full burial rituals. The urn was decorated with symbols commemorating his life and Zuboko had protected it with a spell.

Cruntck's memory was marked by a head stone. The heroes had been unable to retrieve his remains as they had blown away on the wind, but he would be in their hearts for ever.

Sorrowfully, the heroes left the memorials and walked together to the derelict meeting room. "We cannot delay any longer!" Harthor spoke sternly. "We need to return to our quest of defeating Ladracsin."

"Harthor's right!" Lexon commented, "We still need to reach Rakshar"

"I know, but what do we do with the city of Krakara?" Aerlyn asked.

Zuboko pondered. "The city never had any honour; I think we should dispose of it!"

"Are you suggesting that we destroy the city?" roared Lexon.

"Zuboko is right. There is so much evil in this city now that any creature that comes here could become a deadly successor to Numbar" Harthor replied.

The four slowly nodded their heads in tacit agreement.

Gathering their provisions, Lexon, Aerlyn, Harthor and Zuboko walked purposefully to the perimeter of the city and stood gazing at the fallen ruins of the once mighty city. Aerlyn and Lexon took up their bows and Zuboko and Harthor lit the arrows with flaming torches. Simultaneously, they released the arrows which flew into the night sky like shooting stars. Reaching their targets, the fire took hold and spread quickly and intensely devouring the city and, with it, the remains of all that was once evil.

Watching as the flames licked at the central tower, Zuboko's eyes were drawn upwards to the black of the night sky. There, in the stars, was the smiling face of Mollynia. In an instant, her mouth moved to motion the word "Goodbye!" Bitter tears scorched Zuboko's eyes.

The heroes turned and made their way quietly into the darkness; they had restarted the long journey to Rakshar and were ready to confront whatever troubles may await them.

Hours later, long after the heroes had departed, the last smoldering flames died away leaving nothing but ash where the once mighty city had stood.

Only one feature remained; the memorials to those that had died fighting for the rebellion lay untouched and undamaged by the mystical fire and stood proud, silhouetted against the rising sun.

. Epilogue .

"No! No! Please, I beg of you, no more, no more! Aaaarrrgh!" screeched Numbar as his evil soul was repeatedly tortured, deep within the torment and fires of hell.

Ladracsin was unforgiving, "Congratulations Numbar! Your soul is mine and you will spend eternity here for failing to kill those fools."

"Oh Master, I am sorry! Give me another chance! Aaaarrgh!" The last echoes of Numbar's howls were heard as he plummeted into the fiery depths of hell.

Printed in the United Kingdom
by Lightning Source UK Ltd.
R617000001B/R6170PG116269UKSX1B/1-51

9 781846 853975